Maboroshi

Mari Okada

YEN ON

New York

MARI OKADA

Translation by Amelia Imogen

maboroshi

First published in Japan in 2023 by KADOKAWA CORPORATION, Tokyo.
English translation rights arranged with KADOKAWA CORPORATION, Tokyo through
TUTTLE-MORI AGENCY, INC., Tokyo.

Yen On
150 West 30th Street, 6th Floor
New York, NY 10001

Visit us at yenpress.com • facebook.com/yenpress • twitter.com/yenpress
yenpress.tumblr.com • instagram.com/yenpress

First Yen On Edition: March 2025
Edited by Yen On Editorial: Leilah Labossiere
Designed by Yen Press Design: Lilliana Checo

Yen On is an imprint of Yen Press, LLC.
The Yen On name and logo are trademarks of Yen Press, LLC.

Library of Congress Cataloging-in-Publication Data is available.

ISBNs: 979-8-8554-0775-4 (hardcover)
979-8-8554-0776-1 (ebook)

10 9 8 7 6 5 4 3 2 1

LSC-C

Printed in the United States of America

Most of the people who lived in Mifuse worked at the steel factory.

That included Masamune Kikuiri's father, grandfather, and uncle. Everybody worked there, without exception. Unless another strong desire awakened within him, Masamune would probably follow the same path.

New Mifuse Steel Factory was built on a skinny piece of land when Masamune's grandfather was still young. It was thanks to that factory that the town attracted people from other places, but no matter how much the town prospered, the only new establishments that opened were bars that catered to factory workers. There were barely any recreational facilities for kids, and a certain sense of desolation still lingered in the air. That said, simply being born in Mifuse seemed to provide people with a wealth of connections when it came to job hunting, and life was pretty comfortable there. As a result, everyone had this vaguely carefree and unambitious attitude toward life.

The steel factory constantly puffed out smoke.

If that wasn't bad enough, the area didn't get much fresh air, either. It was bordered by mountains on one side, and the view of the sea was hindered by an inlet. The smoke from the steel factory was born and died in the town, as if it were crematorium smoke for all the people who'd spent their entire lives in Mifuse. At least, that was how it looked through the lens of a middle school student like Masamune.

* * *

That night, however, the smoke was different.

"This one's from a listener who calls themselves Sleepy Lamb: 'I've had enough of studying for my entrance exam. Someone help me. I feel like I'm dying.'"

That day, Masamune Kikuiri and his friends were studying for their entrance exams.

They were sitting at a table with a heater underneath—called a *kotatsu*—idling the time away as the radio played in the background. Sasakura, the chubby jokester of the group, was reading manga without the slightest bit of shame.

"You've gotta live in the now! Take this—philosophical secret technique: Energeia!"

He slammed himself into Senba. Slender and meek-looking, Senba was the total opposite of Sasakura.

"That hurts. Geez, can't you just knuckle down and study?"

The DJ continued reading out the listener's message in his distinctive, high-pitched voice. The radio program reverberated around the room.

"'It feels like I have no escape right now. There's nothin' I dream of becoming, and I have no interest in the future, either. I feel like I'm stuck in an endless tunnel of darkness.'"

Nitta, who—likely due to his much older brother's influence—acted and dressed maturely for his age, snorted with laughter.

"Why bother sending such an irrelevant complaint to a radio station?" he said. "They make it sound like entrance exams are a life-and-death situation. That's so dumb."

There were three high schools in Mifuse. There was an all-girls high school with an ugly uniform and a technical high school where the clothes were equally unfashionable. Then there was the ordinary high school. Very few of the students who attended went on to university. Unless someone was hoping to go to a school outside Mifuse, the entrance exams weren't that difficult.

"Aren't you gonna go to university, Nitta?"

"Haven't decided yet. What about you, Senba?"

"I… Well, I'll go wherever. I mean, if I'm going to end up at the steel factory anyway…"

"What? Not much of a dreamer, are ya?" said Sasakura, raising his hands in an exaggerated show of dismay.

"Well, what do *you* want to do in the future, Sasakura?"

"Me? I'm gonna be Mutsumi Sagami's kept man!"

Masamune, who'd stayed quiet until then, started to shake with laughter. Nitta let out another exasperated snort.

"What's her appeal supposed to be? She's such a plain Jane," he said.

"She seems like a total pushover. Who can resist that? Push and shove, push and shove!"

Sasakura was always starting fights with Senba.

"That hurts!" Senba exclaimed.

While everyone else was joking around, Masamune turned his face away, looking sulky. Whenever Mutsumi Sagami came up in conversation, Masamune—who had long hair and androgynous features—would develop a menacing glare.

As Nitta had suggested, Mutsumi wasn't a girl who stood out. She wasn't ugly—she was slightly taller than the other girls and had a narrow, pretty nose—but she always smiled shyly and never put herself out there.

When Masamune replayed Mutsumi's voice in his head, he could only recall her saying typical stuff like "Hey, stop it" or "Oh, really?" She'd giggle with the other girls as they fawned over drawings of male anime characters, but her laughter was always slightly softer than those around her.

None of these behaviors seemed actively malicious, but for some reason, every little thing she did got on Masamune's nerves.

"Well, no matter what your goal is, there's one important thing we can't forget! Each and every one of us was born to be happy…," Sasakura declared in a theatrical tone before grabbing a snack from the *kotatsu* table and triumphantly shouting the product's name. "Happy Turn!"

Then, *plllbbbbttt*. Sasakura let out a loud and perfectly timed fart—although the blanket of the *kotatsu* muffled the noise a little.

"Ahhhh!" everyone yelled in unison as they scrambled out from beneath the table.

"What the heck?! You can't fart underneath a *kotatsu*!"

"Ugh, I spilled my juice!"

"Is your stomach rotting or something? It smells like pickles…"

Masamune hastily opened the window to let some fresh air in—but at that very moment, he was hit by a shock wave so strong that it almost knocked him off his feet. The intense shaking was immediately followed by a deep, thunderous roar that seemed to reverberate through his abdomen.

"Wait, what…?"

"Whoa, look at that!"

When the boys looked up, they saw a dark red flickering light coming from the direction of the steel factory. The factory was engulfed in flames, painting the dark, starry sky crimson. Then black smoke began to billow out, spreading rapidly and creating a gradient of color in the smoky night sky.

"A fire?!"

"N-no way. Are your dads gonna be okay?!"

Sasakura's father ran an electrical appliance store. Nitta's and Senba's fathers both worked at the steel factory. There was no sign that Akimune, Masamune's father, had come home yet, either.

Masamune could hear his heart pounding. He began to sweat—and it was freezing cold, too. The radio DJ continued reading out the message, oblivious to the situation unfolding in Mifuse.

"But if I get into high school, I'm gonna change. I'm gonna dye my hair and work hard in my club activities, and I'll even write in my journal every day. So…"

"Aghhhhh?!"

The red glow enveloping the steel factory had expanded dramatically, filling the sky above Mifuse. Suddenly, there was a flash of light, suggesting something had caught fire. For a moment, all that Masamune and his friends could see was white…

…Before he knew it, Masamune and the others were back underneath the *kotatsu*.

No juice had spilled, and the Happy Turn snacks were sitting unopened on the table.

Masamune and his friends were frozen in place, unable to move a finger. They didn't have a clue what had just happened, but it felt as though there was something they were intensely cognizant of. Hoping for a clue, they were reluctant to disturb the air in any way.

The infuriating ticking sound of the owl-shaped wall clock's moving eyes echoed around the room.

"It feels like I have no escape right now."

The boys exchanged glances. It was as though they were glaring at one another with probing looks in their eyes. The radio spewed out the exact same sentence the boys had heard moments earlier.

"But if I get into high school, I'm gonna change."

These words spurred the boys to lift their heads and run out of the room.

"Masamune!"

As the boys were pulling on their shoes at the entrance, Masamune's mother—Misato—emerged from the living room with a tense expression on her face.

"Are you leaving?" she asked.

Misato seemed to know something, too. Masamune gave her a small nod and opened the sliding door in the entryway.

"A crack…?"

Huge fissures had split the winter night sky, as though it were a mirror that someone had dropped.

The fissures were emitting a tremendously nerve-racking cracking sound…as they spread farther and farther. The light shining through the gaps was bizarrely awe-inspiring.

"…Oh…"

The line Masamune had heard on the radio was spinning around and around inside his head.

"*But if I get into high school, I'm gonna change. I'm gonna dye my hair and work hard in my club activities, and I'll even write in my journal every day. So…*'"

Having recalled that much of it, Masamune muttered quietly to himself.

"So…I'm begging you, God."

Then the smoke coming from the steel factory started twisting and turning, before assuming the shape of living creatures. It almost looked like a bunch of dragons… No, that wasn't it.

They're wolves, Masamune thought.

The texture of the smoke resembled bristled fur, and it looked like it was soaring across the sky in a pack. The smoke slicing through the wind sounded like a wolf howling in the distance.

"…?!"

Then the pack of wolves in the sky abruptly changed direction, hurtling down at breakneck speed. One of them bared its fangs and charged directly toward Masamune and his friends.

"Waaaah!"

The smoke wolf came dangerously close to Masamune and his companions as it rushed by. The intense wind pressure seemed to tear at their hair and clothes. They dropped to the ground, trying to shield themselves from it.

"Oh."

The pack of wolves had scattered far and wide, seemingly making a show of their progress. Then they began to ascend rapidly toward the cracks appearing all over the sky.

The smoke wolves sank their teeth into the fissures. They weren't biting them so much as trying to infiltrate the crevices. Once they'd done so, the cracks sealed back up—as if they'd been filled in with putty—and let out a hissing noise as they vanished from sight. At the same time, the smoke wolves evaporated, enveloping the area in nothing but jet-black darkness.

Although Masamune didn't really understand anything that was happening, there was one thing he was certain of.

No god was going to grant their wishes.

*

Recently, something called the "fainting game" had gained popularity among Masamune Kikuiri's peers.

First, they got ready by squatting down and taking several exaggerated deep breaths. Once their lungs were full of air, they immediately stood up and crossed their arms in front of their chest. Then somebody wrapped their arms around the person's middle from behind and squeezed hard.

"One, two, three!"

With that, the person would abruptly lose consciousness.

The tenuous connection to the continuous flow of time that they'd had since birth—even while asleep—was brusquely interrupted.

When Masamune snapped back to his senses, he found Sasakura and the others looking down at him and laughing.

"He just went *buheh. Buheh!*"

"Oh, his pupils are back to normal."

He didn't remember losing consciousness or making a *buheh* sound. He knew they were talking about him, but it certainly didn't feel like it. Wiping away a trickle of blood from his nose with the back of his hand, he looked around. Yellowish floaters in his vision stood out against the sooty white wall of the unremarkable school building.

He cast aside any certainty he'd once felt regarding his own existence.

For Masamune, this was the most exhilarating game he could play. Although it had been banned by their teachers, Masamune and his friends continued to secretly indulge in it behind the school building.

Masamune stayed crumpled on the floor. Despite regaining consciousness, he still felt dazed. That period of haziness was something other people weren't supposed to encroach on. As usual, Sasakura and the others left him alone.

"Who's going next?"

"I almost died the other day, you know!"

Masamune looked up, ignoring the other boys' chatter. Beyond brown trees, he could see the rusty fence of the school roof. A figure with slender legs stood behind the mesh fencing.

It was Mutsumi Sagami.

She was wearing a snug pair of short socks. The acute angle of her partially visible ankles appeared to emphasize what a clean-cut girl Mutsumi was—a pure maiden who excelled in math and maintained a perfectly upright posture.

She'd always seemed like an inconspicuous, timid girl, but the impression Masamune used to have of her had already faded into obscurity. When she noticed his gaze, Mutsumi gave him a startlingly cold look. It was completely different from the lethargic smile she usually had around her friends. And that wasn't all.

"Aren't you worried about me seeing your underwear…?"

"Huh? Did you say something about underwear? Did you pee your pants, Masamune?" Sasakura joked, but Masamune wasn't listening.

He got the impression that Mutsumi was making fun of him. She didn't see him as a guy.

With her lips slightly parted, Mutsumi gave Masamune, who was completely captivated by her, an acknowledgement. Then she vanished out of sight before Sasakura and the others noticed her presence. The moment she descended the rusty staircase and stepped foot into the corridor again, she would disguise herself as a wholly unremarkable young girl.

It was homeroom period, at the end of the day. The teacher hadn't shown up, so the classroom was abuzz with chatter.

"That's not what I mean," said Sasakura, his gaze fixed on Mutsumi Sagami. He was chatting to Nitta in a deliberately loud voice.

As it turned out, Sasakura's staring had been far too obvious.

"Uhh, Mutsumi. He's staring at you," one girl whispered in Mutsumi's ear. The girl, whose name was Yasumi, had a honey-sweet voice and a petite build.

"No, he isn't," replied Mutsumi, bashfully shaking her head.

Hara—the class president—scowled, visibly annoyed.

"Is Sasakura stupid or something?" she said. "He's acting like he's in heat."

"What's the issue?" Yasumi chimed in. "Hey, why don't you just give him a wave?"

"Come on. It's not like that… Save me, Sonobe!"

Begging for help, Mutsumi threw her arms around Sonobe, who was sitting next to her. Sonobe was a girl with short, bristly hair and sturdy shoulders. She gave Mutsumi a vague smile, but her eyes remained expressionless.

When Sasakura saw how Mutsumi was acting, he looked pleased with himself.

"That's so cute. She's embarrassed," he said.

As Masamune watched the interaction out of the corner of his eye, his heart grew cold. At that moment, the door clattered open, and the teacher walked in.

"Hey. Who forgot to hand in their self-monitoring form? Hurry up and give it to me."

As Masamune played dumb and stared out of the window, the teacher homed in on him.

"I'm talking about you, Kikuiri. Your self-monitoring form!"

* * *

At dusk, the steel factory tirelessly puffed out smoke. Masamune and his friends were sitting on a levee, eating ice cream—even though it was winter.

"You're such an overthinker, Masamune. Just write whatever you want on that form," Nitta said, prompting Masamune to hang his head.

"Easier said than done… I mean, what *do* I want to be in the future?"

"It's simple. Just say you want to work at New Mifuse Steel Factory."

Masamune gave a half-hearted response: "I guess so."

"I wonder what Sagami wrote. Maybe she wants to be a TV presenter," Sasakura said, butting in.

"No way. She's too plain for that," one of Masamune's friends retorted.

"She seems like she'd struggle in front of other people," said another.

Masamune almost snickered at how little they knew about Mutsumi.

"Anyway, she'd never be able to do anything like that. You need a university degree to become a TV presenter, so she'd never make it," Nitta declared.

Mutsumi had decent grades, but nobody challenged Nitta's assertion that she'd never get into university. That was the kind of pessimism that the town of Mifuse instilled in a person.

"Hey, wanna fly? It's been a while since we last tried it," Sasakura suggested, trying to lighten the mood.

He stood up on the levee and shouted, "Here I go!" He pretended to flap his arms before jumping off it.

"Whoa, I hope you fall on your head!"

Masamune silently followed Sasakura's lead, gently jumping off the levee and landing on the ground below.

There was a vague stinging sensation underneath his feet. Before the fainting game was popular, they used to jump from all sorts of things—tetrapod structures, levees, and even parking lot roofs.

"Yeah," he muttered, savoring the pain as he looked up at the mountains. They looked like something out of an oil painting. Despite it being winter, they were still covered in sections of green.

"My breath's white today…," he observed, watching his visible puff of breath drift up into the air. In the background, an even denser mass of hazy white smoke was swirling around.

"Oh, it's a wolf."

A siren blared from the steel factory.

The smoke released by the factory assumed the shape of a wolf, just as it had *that* day. At some point, everybody—not just Masamune—had started calling these smoke clouds "wolves." The wolf drifted away with a howl. If they followed the wolves' trail, they'd soon discover that small fissures had appeared in the sky. Thanks to the wolves' excellent sense of smell, they could sniff out even the tiniest cracks that Masamune and his friends wouldn't notice.

Once the wolves bit into those tiny cracks, the sky went back to its original state—and the siren stopped.

The wolves disappeared as if they'd never been there at all, and so did the pain-like sensation in Masamune's feet.

It was a winter night in the countryside. A heavy darkness had fallen, and though they could hear insects flapping their wings, there was no other sign of life—just the buzzing of an old streetlamp.

In the small space in front of a narrow entrance, seemingly meaning-less decorations were on display. It wasn't clear what they were supposed to express, nor who was supposed to see them. Masamune, having returned home, opened the door—which was adorned with a tacky grape relief carving—and muttered, "I'm back."

"Dinner's ready, Masamune," his mother, Misato, called from the kitchen.

When he glanced into the living room, he met eyes with Tokimune. The man was sipping *shochu*.

"Hey, welcome back," said Tokimune.

"Oh, Uncle Tokimune."

Tokimune was Masamune's dad's brother. He was relaxing under the *kotatsu*, still wearing his steel factory uniform. Masamune's grandfather,

Souji, was sitting on a legless chair on the floor, his back hunched. Souji was always in this spot, apart from late at night, when he spent his time staring intently at the TV, which only played the same old dramas and the same old news shows.

"Okay. We're having ginger pork today."

In the Kikuiri household, they ate the same few meals in rotation: dumplings, simmered fish, teriyaki fish, teriyaki chicken, ginger pork, and sausages stir-fried in sauce. Although Misato rarely deviated from this list of options, she never failed to announce, "We're having X today." Still, there was one fundamental issue.

"Our ginger pork has no ginger in it. Isn't it garlic pork?"

Masamune's casual question made Misato wave her hand dismissively.

"As long as it looks like ginger pork, there's no real difference."

"Yeah! My sister-in-law's right," Tokimune said facetiously, earning him a piercing glare from Misato.

"You need to let us know when you're coming, Tokimune. I only made two cups of rice."

"No stress. This is good enough for me…," said Tokimune, lifting his empty *shochu* glass.

At that moment, a voice shouting *"Wait!"* came from the grainy TV screen. There was a detective show on—one that Souji watched all the time. Standing in the pouring rain, the tearful-looking detective was yelling at a woman whose vibes basically screamed "criminal."

"I want to know everything!" he said.

"I want to know everything," Masamune muttered under his breath, repeating the line for no real reason—but no one noticed him.

"Oh, I almost forgot. You left the garden faucet on again, Souji, didn't you?"

Souji responded to Misato's complaint with a noncommittal grunt.

Tokimune mimicked him, making a similar noise as he raised his empty glass.

"Seriously, the men in this house…"

* * *

After dinner, Masamune found himself in his room staring blankly at his self-monitoring form.

Everyone in Mifuse—regardless of age or gender—was required to regularly fill out these forms. They asked for inoffensive information like age, gender, blood type, and address, but also detailed descriptions of what he liked, who he liked, and even less concrete things that were hard to put into words, such as subtle changes in his feelings.

Ideally, these responses remained unchanged.

Change meant drifting away from one's true self. There was an original version of a person, and if they didn't cling to it, they could slowly become a fake.

Masamune started doodling on the edge of the form. The drawing depicted a boy clutching his knees against his chest, wrapped in thorns that dug into his skin. It was the typical kind of drawing an angsty teenager would do, but the obsessive level of detail that Masamune was adding made it look more and more lifelike. Masamune had been inspired by the illustrator of an RPG he liked, and he'd begun to enjoy replicating their Western style.

"Hey."

Tokimune, who'd just come out of the bath, entered the room with a cigarette in hand. Masamune hurriedly turned his self-monitoring form over.

Tokimune took a seat on the balcony and pulled the old tin ashtray that had been left there toward him. After lighting his cigarette, he frowned, seemingly repulsed by the taste.

"They're supposed to be immoral, alcohol and cigarettes. I thought you were doing God's work," Masamune remarked.

"That factory runs itself... All we do is pretend to work. We have a morning assembly, conduct a few inspections here and there..."

Tokimune let out a puff of cigarette smoke. The smoke trail drifted in the direction of the steel factory. It was still running—even though it was nighttime, and there couldn't be any workers there.

"…and then we check where the smoke goes. That's about it." Masamune snorted disinterestedly. Tokimune smiled blithely and continued speaking. "You were drawing, weren't you…? Why don't you do the illustrations for the steel factory's monthly report?"

Masamune flinched, then let out an exaggerated sigh.

"It feels weird when you go out of your way to be considerate."

"Kids like you are so—"

Masamune interrupted Tokimune, not wanting to hear his response.

"I'm not a kid," he stated. "Still, there's nothing that makes me want to be an adult, either."

This left Tokimune speechless. At that moment, a shrill siren reverberated from the steel factory again. Smoke emerged from the building. It looked gray during the day, but in the darkness, the smoke appeared to have a white fur-like texture. The smoke wolves headed for the small cracks in the sky.

The fissures glimmered a deep shade of blue-green, scattered with yellow and pink, but they were soon filled up by the smoke.

"Wasn't that the second time today? It's been happening a lot lately…," Tokimune murmured, but Masamune had no intention of responding.

*

The next day, a minor incident occurred at school.

Sonobe wasn't wearing her inside shoes.

She'd been sitting in the classroom since early that morning, hiding her feet, so initially, Masamune was the only person who noticed. Hara, the leader of the group of girls, was the one who eventually changed that.

"Ew, Sonobe. What's going on here?!" she shrieked.

From then on, everyone's attention was drawn to Sonobe's feet. The soles of her white socks were covered in dust and dirt.

The teacher, who'd arrived while this commotion was unfolding, began to question Sonobe. Sonobe's voice was muffled and hard to hear, but when Hara and Yasumi started shouting "How terrible!" and "Who did that?!" it became obvious that someone had stolen Sonobe's indoor shoes. Like the other girls, Mutsumi was rubbing Sonobe's back and looking concerned.

"Are you okay, Sonobe?" she asked.

"This is bullying, isn't it?" Sasakura suddenly declared.

He was a real rarity—the kind of person who could highlight a fact so obvious that everyone else in the room was already aware of it.

Sasakura's statement made Sonobe burst into tears, covering her face with her hands.

This prompted all the girls to begin a tirade about how terrible the perpetrator was, how cowardly it was not to come forward, and how what they'd done was totally unforgivable.

Mutsumi kept her hand on Sonobe's back the whole time—but to Masamune, it seemed like there was a little more to it.

At lunchtime, Masamune—along with Sasakura and the others—went to the back of the school building to play their usual fainting game. In truth, though, Masamune wasn't in the mood for it.

"Oh, we're safe. The teacher's gone. Want to have a go, Masamune?"

Sasakura wrapped his arms around Masamune from behind.

Masamune, lacking enthusiasm, crossed his arms in front of his chest robotically. Then Sasakura smirked and started fondling Masamune's chest.

"Masamuneeeeee," he crooned in a sickly-sweet voice.

"Stop it!" said Masamune, trying to get away.

"Hey, Sasakura. Don't use Masamune as an outlet for your sexual frustration."

"But when you look at him from behind, he looks so much like a girl."

"You're the chubby one. I bet your boobs are bigger!" Masamune clapped back, prompting Sasakura to fondle his own chest.

"Whoa, so sexy!" he joked.

Nitta and Senba began to laugh, so Masamune found himself doing the same—but when he happened to look up, his smile froze.

* * *

Mutsumi Sagami was standing on the roof, holding the hem of her skirt.

Startled, Masamune hurriedly averted his gaze.

"What's up, Masamune?"

"Uhh, nothing. I'll go later. Somebody else can take my turn."

"Oh. Then I wanna have a go! ♪"

Once his friends had started playing the fainting game again, Masamune looked back up. Mutsumi checked that Masamune was the only one watching, then…subtly hitched up her skirt.

"…?!"

All the blood in Masamune's body rushed not to his groin, but to his head.

Seeing Mutsumi's underwear didn't make him happy. He felt a mix of embarrassment, frustration, and fury. Intense anger surged inside him.

Before he knew it, Masamune started running toward the school building.

"Hey, where are you going?"

"I'll be back in a moment!"

"Back from where?!"

Masamune flung off his outdoor shoes at the entrance, then ran erratically through the hallway. Then he began climbing the emergency staircase that led up to the roof.

The door to the roof always used to be locked, but recently, someone had started leaving it open.

He bolted out onto the roof, kicking a caution cone out of the way in the process. Despite this, Masamune lifted his head defiantly—but Mutsumi Sagami was nowhere to be seen.

Discouraged, Masamune attempted to pick up the cone he'd knocked over. At that moment, however, he spotted something under the nearby water tank—a pair of small indoor shoes.

"……"

Masamune gulped nervously. Mutsumi was the only person who frequented this depressing rooftop—which meant the culprit who stole Sonobe's indoor shoes must have been…

He carefully walked over to the shoes and picked them up—but then he dropped them again, unable to stop himself from going "Ah!" They bounced gently off the ground, then lay still on the roof. There was a name written on the back of each, and it was *Mutsumi Sagami*.

"…Oh! Mutsumi…Sagami."

Sonobe's indoor shoes had gone missing, but these belonged to Sagami.

"—Pervert."

The sudden, casual insult made Masamune flinch.

When he turned around, he found Mutsumi standing behind him. She wasn't wearing the fake smile she always used in the classroom. She had that icy look in her eyes that only Masamune knew.

"Give them back."

"Oh… Uh, sure."

Masamune picked up the indoor shoes and gently tossed them at Mutsumi's feet. Once she had them, she took off the indoor shoes she'd been wearing. She hooked her fingers in the back of them, and with a gentle tug, the shoes slipped off her feet and onto the floor.

"Great. These were a little too big to walk in… Where did you find those?"

"Huh?"

"The shoes."

It was Masamune's first opportunity to have some semblance of a conversation with her, but the only response he could muster was a groan. Once again, he was surprised by what he'd seen.

The name written on the inside of the shoes that Mutsumi had been wearing was Yuuko Sonobe.

"…What's going on here?"

"Sonobe stole my indoor shoes."

"Huh? She stole…your shoes?"

Sonobe was the perpetrator, and Mutsumi was the victim? If that was true, why was Mutsumi wearing Sonobe's shoes? And why was Sonobe crying in the classroom?

Countless questions came to mind, but Masamune couldn't seem to ask them out loud. Mutsumi picked up her indoor shoes, put them on, and tapped the floor with the tips of her toes to make sure they were on well.

"It's just like that fainting game you guys play. It stems from boredom."

As Masamune became more confused, Mutsumi flashed him a mischievous smile.

"Hey… Want me to show you something that will get rid of all your boredom?"

*

Masamune and Mutsumi were about the same height.

Mutsumi, however, was walking at a recklessly brisk pace. She didn't care to slow down for him, so Masamune had to try desperately to keep up.

Mutsumi was making a beeline for the center of Mifuse. Unlike what the term *center* would suggest, there weren't that many shops in the area, nor was it near the station. Everybody just called it that. The center of Mifuse was in the vicinity of the steel factory. Mifuse was structured around the steel factory in every possible way.

After crossing a small, low bridge and passing through an area with little pedestrian traffic, Masamune finally attempted to speak to Mutsumi.

"Where are we going?"

"Well, where do you think?" Mutsumi responded, with a dry laugh. The smile on her face wasn't the one Masamune had seen on the rooftop, nor was it the one she used in the classroom. It seemed somewhat unstable.

It was clear that he was being toyed with. Masamune couldn't figure out why he was silently accompanying her or what he was hoping would happen, but *not* going wasn't an option for him.

Masamune was sure that he hated Mutsumi Sagami. And yet the thought that she might have chosen him in some way made his cheeks go red, even without the sunset lending them its glow.

Once they'd crossed the bridge and walked a little farther, they reached a divided highway that wasn't technically a highway. There were a few houses around, but the only notable commercial establishment was a rest area with a rusty sign. Its main customers were truck drivers delivering to the steel factory, providing them with an opportunity to grab a light meal and take a breather. The rest area was also decked out with arcade machines, making it a popular spot for middle and high school students to hang out after school.

The hot sandwiches sold at the vending machine in the rest area were Masamune's favorite. He loved the ham and cheese sandwiches that were wrapped in aluminum foil. His father had often bought them for him on his way home from work.

"……"

As soon as his father crossed his mind, Masamune's footsteps felt so much heavier—whereas his suspicion and anticipation had seemed to lighten the load before.

Then he recalled the incident that had unfolded in the steel factory. It had only occurred that winter, and yet the accident was from a distant past.

The day that the steel factory explosion occurred.

His father, Akimune, came home late that night. Masamune heard water pouring. He ran downstairs to find Akimune with his head in the sink. The lights were off, and he was simply dousing his head in water. His eyes were vacant, and it was hard to tell what he was looking at.

"What's wrong…?"

"Nothing… I just…feel kind of dirty… Like I've gotten dirty."

This wasn't surprising. If he'd been at the steel factory at the time of the explosion, it was only natural that he would have gotten dirty. And yet Akimune's skin and clothing looked clean—although the lack of light may have been partially to blame for that.

"Did you get caught up in what happened, Dad?"

"Um… I'm not sure, but, well, I guess so," his father responded, not turning off the water.

Masamune got the urge to ask his father what he meant but found himself feeling somewhat unconcerned about the ordeal. No, that wasn't right. Masamune felt like there was no changing the situation, no matter what the details were. Masamune wasn't the only one who felt that way—everybody living in Mifuse felt the same. Despite the magnitude of the accident, there was no real upheaval, and this was just another peaceful night in the countryside.

And yet the whole of Mifuse had taken a strange, albeit quiet, turn.

First of all, phone calls weren't coming through anymore. Or, to be precise, Mifuse could no longer connect to the outside world. Trains stopped arriving. The tunnel had been sealed off by a landslide. People tried to sail out to sea from the port, but even that wasn't possible. For some reason, the sea currents prevented them from leaving.

A disaster prevention meeting was held about the incident, with the mayor at its core. About a week later, the people of Mifuse assembled in the town hall parking lot.

"Now then, in regard to what has happened…"

The mayor, holding a megaphone, explained the situation to the assembled citizens. Since they had only a half day at school, Masamune had gone along with Sasakura and his other friends.

Next to the mayor stood several steel factory employees in uniform. They were all supposed to be workers with managerial posts, but for some reason, Akimune—who was just a regular employee—was there as well.

"We will now hear Mr. Mamoru Sagami's views on the matter. He is a descendant of the family of priests at Mifuse Shrine and an employee of the New Mifuse Steel Factory."

"Hey, isn't that Mutsumi Sagami's dad?" Sasakura whispered to Masamune.

"I think so," Masamune replied.

The tall, lanky man called Mamoru Sagami seemed to be an ordinary employee, just like Akimune. With a mixture of anxiety and elation in his voice, he asked Masamune's father a question.

"Should I go ahead, Akimune?" he said.

Akimune responded with a somewhat sad smile.

"Yes, please."

Megaphone in hand, Mr. Sagami climbed onto the platform that had been set up in the parking lot.

"Thank you for introducing me," he began, but the screeching feedback from the speaker made a small child cover their ears. "Um, well… We, the people of Mifuse, have lived off the benefits of the iron extracted from Kanzari Mountain since the Industrial Revolution…"

Mr. Sagami spoke hesitantly, but no one made fun of him or looked bored. They watched him intently, hanging on to his every word—as though they were hoping for validation. With so many earnest gazes directed toward him, Mr. Sagami's eyes gradually began to sparkle, and his voice grew more confident.

"However, what we worship at Mifuse Shrine is the mountain itself. You could even say that the people of Mifuse have been whittling away at their god for many years… Yes, I know why this incident happened!" Mr. Sagami, who was now fully in the swing of things, flared his nostrils as he made his assertion. "It was divine punishment!"

Everyone was at a loss for words. Pure, undiluted silence filled the parking lot—but it didn't take long for it to be shattered.

"Wha…what do you mean, punishment?" a middle-aged man cried, prompting other citizens to speak their minds as well.

"That doesn't make any sense. What's that guy talking about?"

"Didn't you know? The only son of the Sagami family is well-known for being a weirdo…"

This reaction made Mr. Sagami's eyes bulge, and he shouted even louder.

"I guess ignorance is bliss, is it?!"

Mr. Sagami's bizarrely ferocious attitude left everyone speechless again. He was addressing the crowd at such a volume that it was almost impossible to believe how hesitant he'd been at the start.

"The steel factory you see today isn't the same factory that stood there before. That explosion was a turning point—and it has transformed. It's now a machine created not by Buddha, but by our god. A Sacred Machine!"

People began to stir. Masamune looked at his dad in desperation. Akimune, who was always laid-back and easygoing, had a blank expression on his face.

Mr. Sagami, who was basking in the limelight, continued to shout. He sounded completely bewitched.

"This Sacred Machine has trapped us in the town of Mifuse!"

Mamoru Sagami was the heir to Mifuse Shrine. He seemed to be an ordinary employee at the steel factory, but the bizarre situation Mifuse found itself in couldn't be explained by common sense alone. In this unprecedented situation, Mamoru—who was known more for twisting logic to explain mysterious happenings than for actually understanding them—ended up gaining people's trust. Despite being the heir to the small shrine, he had no choice but to work at the steel factory to support himself.

Mamoru claimed that the town's citizens hadn't been transported to another world like in science fiction stories, nor were they repeating the same day time and time again. According to him, they'd been trapped in Mifuse as a punishment for continuously mining the sacred mountain where the god resided. Once the deity's mood improved, the world would go back to the way it was.

Some people questioned why the priest—if his theory was true—was willing to work at the steel factory in the first place. Still, Mr. Sagami wasn't fazed by such criticisms, declaring that he would use his status as the priest to protect the steel factory, which had now turned into a Sacred Machine. And that's exactly what happened.

Akimune, whom Mr. Sagami was particularly fond of, became his right-hand man. Mr. Sagami—with his peculiar way of speaking and disregard for social cues—had always been an outsider, ridiculed by his coworkers. Akimune was the only one who treated him normally.

As Mr. Sagami gained authority at the steel factory, Akimune's standing also rose. Despite this, Akimune seemed to be suffering. He even started missing work regularly. And then…

"We're here."

Mutsumi's announcement brought Masamune's train of thought to a sudden halt.

When he hastily looked up, he was awestruck. They were at the steel factory.

When he looked at it from far away, it loomed menacingly in the distance, backed by the iron mine. Up close, it was rusty and red, so enormous that it was impossible to deduce its true scale. The steel factory exuded an eerie, almost horror-like atmosphere. Mutsumi hadn't been leading Masamune to a place near the steel factory—she'd been taking him to the factory itself.

"H-hey. The grown-ups will be furious if they find out we're here…," said Masamune.

"Don't be silly," Mutsumi replied.

Disregarding his hesitation, she made her way to what seemed to be a back entrance for vehicles. Although the iron gate was shut tight, the small door beside it had been left unlocked, and Mutsumi easily slipped inside.

"Hey!" Masamune called out as she walked away—but she wasn't going to stop just because he said so.

"…Dammit. Why am I such an idiot?"

For a moment, Masamune thought about turning back, but he couldn't bring himself to do it. He was determined not to reveal any trivial uncertainty or fear that might disappoint Mutsumi. That was something he wanted to avoid at all costs.

What lay ahead was going to eradicate his boredom.

As he stepped onto the factory site, he noticed a few employees wandering around, but they didn't seem to be working. They were simply smoking or sitting idly, and they paid no attention to the two youths as Mutsumi continued to advance farther inside.

The working blast furnaces were making loud clanging noises, with smoke belching out from their surroundings. When he'd seen it from afar, Masamune had sort of assumed that the smoke was released from the chimneys, but that wasn't the case. Steam was rising from the floor and walls.

Still, Masamune got the overpowering impression that something was missing. Life, maybe. Despite all the trees on the mountain behind the factory, there were no birdcalls to be heard.

Mutsumi arrived at one of the massive blast furnaces right at the back of the steel factory. It was the only one that wasn't in operation. Fenced off with barbed wire, it was perfectly silent. Without pause, Mutsumi stepped over the barbed wire and went inside. Then she opened the door. It must have been rusty, because it creaked.

Inside was a vast, empty concrete space. Exposed pipes meandered across the ceiling like snakes. Dust had accumulated, but it felt less like a place abandoned for years and more like one where upkeep had simply been lax. The pipes glistened in the light of the setting sun, which streamed in through a giant window.

Masamune felt an overwhelming sense of unease. He looked around, unable to identify what was causing this sensation, but all he spotted was something fluttering amid the sparkling dust that drifted through the air. It was a butterfly.

"Why is there a butterfly here…?"

Masamune hadn't seen a butterfly in a very long time. It was only upon seeing the creature—which was abnormal to encounter during the winter—that he realized what was so strange about the place.

Although the other blast furnaces were in operation, the area around them had felt so lifeless. And yet *this* spot was different—he could sense the staggering pressure of life.

"Hey… Do you…?"

Click. Someone suddenly flicked a switch, and the corner—an area that the sunlight hadn't reached—was illuminated by the harsh, cold light of a mercury vapor lamp. Even though it was only illuminating a small area, its sudden brilliance left Masamune slightly dazed.

It shone down on something resembling a small room in a corner of the blast furnace. It was far from ordinary. Like the rest of the furnace, the ceiling was covered with pipes and the walls were lined with intimidating-looking electrical panels. And yet there was a rug on the floor and an old but well-made velvet sofa in there. Most strange of all, however, there was a peculiar mirror.

Masamune could see Mutsumi's reflection in the mirror. This reflected version of Mutsumi, however, was wearing a casual white dress that showed a lot of skin. Unlike the Mutsumi Masamune knew, this version of her emitted a vaguely gentle aura. Basking in the orange light of sunset, her outline looked indistinct.

Masamune was captivated by her beauty—but then he finally realized something.

The version of Mutsumi he'd believed to be a reflection was in fact…

"Oh…!"

…a girl who bore a striking resemblance to Mutsumi.

The similarity was so uncanny that he'd mistaken the other girl for a reflection in a mirror.

But what was going on? Masamune was confused. Why was a person living in a place like this? And most importantly, why had Mutsumi brought him there?

The girl was staring intently at him. He couldn't bring himself to move.

Masamune's head was spinning—and before he knew it, the girl had moved to within twenty centimeters of him. He gasped; his voice caught in the back of his throat.

The girl—who was now close enough to touch—stared fixedly at Masamune, sniffing his cheeks, hair, and his ears. And then…

"Huh, wait… Wahhh!"

The girl had tried to wrap her arms around Masamune's neck—but then she tripped over and fell into a puddle of water that had collected on the floor.

With that, she let out a strange, enthusiastic yell—although it wasn't clear what was so enjoyable about the situation.

"Gaaahhh!"

This girl was nothing like Mutsumi Sagami.

With her radiant, carefree smile, she was…

…extremely stinky.

Masamune automatically turned his face away. The girl—who'd been inhaling Masamune's own scent—was emitting a cloying, sticky, and rancid stench.

At that moment, Mutsumi let out an intimidating shout and clapped her hands. Startled, the girl scampered to the corner of the room, moving in a beast-like yet agile manner.

Mutsumi silently went over to her. Without giving the girl—who had a fearful look in her eyes—a word of warning, Mutsumi quickly began to take off the girl's one-piece dress.

"…! Hey, wait a moment. Sagami…"

"Kyahhhh!"

The strange girl started to lash out a little, but Mutsumi continued what she was doing without saying a word. It was as though she'd done it a thousand times before. When the dress was off, a dazzling mass of pale skin burst into view. All Masamune could do was look away.

*　*　*

Splash!

Masamune couldn't help but grimace as he used a hose to wash the chamber pot at the water station in the furnace.

"Ugh… That stinks," he grumbled to himself.

Mutsumi was boiling some water in a large kettle, that frigid expression on her face. Next to her, the dress that she'd taken off the girl was soaking in detergent in a metal basin.

"You weren't as surprised as I thought you'd be," she said.

"I was so shocked that my head nearly spun all the way around. What's up with her?"

The girl they'd encountered a short while earlier was currently making loud chewing noises as she devoured sandwiches and fried chicken that Mutsumi had brought her. Although she wasn't eating with her hands, she was gripping her fork with a fist, proving that she hadn't been taught proper manners.

Masamune couldn't bring himself to look directly at her. She was in her underwear, after all. Although she was slim, her body had a softness and smoothness to it. Despite her childish behavior, Masamune was intensely aware that she belonged to the opposite sex.

"She looks like you. Are you sisters or something?"

"Cut it out—that's gross. Take a closer look. We don't look that much alike."

"What's her name?"

"She doesn't have one."

Masamune was surprised by Mutsumi's detached response.

"…So what is she, then?"

"What does she look like to you? A monkey, a gorilla, a chimpanzee?"

When Masamune glanced sideways, he saw that the girl had seemingly lost interest in her food. Having thrown down her fork, she was leaning forward and staring at something.

She was watching the butterfly that Masamune had spotted earlier.

She attempted to catch it, but the butterfly slipped through her fingers. Annoyed, she made a bizarre *ow-ow* sound. Though she looked about the same age as Masamune and Mutsumi, she probably couldn't speak.

Masamune felt like he'd seen a girl like her somewhere before…and then he suddenly remembered where.

That's right—it was a long time ago. He'd seen a feature on TV before they'd been trapped inside Mifuse. It was a story from the distant past about a baby who was raised by wolves that took her in after she was abandoned in a forest. While she looked human, she was a feral child, and she perceived things in a completely different way from other people… Yes, that was the answer Masamune was looking for.

"She seems like a wolf girl, if anything…," Masamune muttered without thinking it through.

"Huh?" replied Mutsumi, looking up at him.

"Oh, nothing… Is this okay?"

Mutsumi watched Masamune put down the chamber pot and nodded firmly.

"Anyway, we can't let her out. That's why I'm stuck taking care of her. She's so big, though—just giving her a bath is hard enough."

Masamune's cheeks flushed. He'd finally realized why Mutsumi was boiling water.

Without missing a beat, Mutsumi continued rambling on.

"I need a boy to help me out and lend me their strength, but I wouldn't want them to get any ideas. It'd cause too much of a nuisance…," she said. "That's why I asked you. You look like a girl."

"Huh?!"

Mutsumi grinned mischievously.

"You like it when Sasakura fondles your chest, after all."

"N-no I don't! Enough with that crap!"

"It doesn't suit you, using crude language out of nowhere."

"I'm going home!"

Masamune started to march away—but after a few steps, he found the wild girl standing in front of him, holding a ball.

"Kyahhh!" she cried out with joy. She seemed to have presumed that he was going to play with her.

"Ugh," grumbled Masamune, coming to a halt.

The girl's skin was extremely pale. Unexplainable dirt and scratches—along with her veins—created patterns across parts of her skin.

"Hmm… Ahh."

The girl grinned at Masamune, who was too stunned to move. Her smile had a formidable brilliance to it, like a flash of light—and it was as warm as sunshine.

For a moment, he'd mistaken her for Mutsumi's reflection in the mirror…but her smile proved that she was a totally different girl. Mutsumi would never have been able to smile like her, no matter how hard she strained her facial muscles…

"It's done boiling. Take it." Mutsumi thrust the kettle toward Masamune, ignoring the girl. "Fill the bathtub with hot water. Dilute it with some cold water, at a ratio of about three to one."

Masamune didn't like being pushed around, but it seemed easier to comply than to confront her head-on. So Masamune followed Mutsumi's command.

He could hear somebody flapping around as he was perfecting the temperature of the water. He became uneasy, sensing that something was happening behind him. Then Mutsumi called him by name.

"Kikuiri."

He reflexively turned around—to find the girl standing there, stark naked.

Masamune froze, dazed. Her limbs were so thin they looked like they could have snapped, but the gentle curves of her body were indisputably feminine. There was an uncompromising flawlessness to her, along with a quiet sense of tension. It was hard to believe that the foul-smelling odor had been produced by her body. Her protruding nipples were a soft shade of pale pink, seamlessly blending into her soft skin, and her belly button was the shape of a gentle downward brushstroke.

Masamune automatically averted his eyes, but Mutsumi grabbed him firmly by the wrist, commanding him to stay in place. Then, after casually checking the temperature of the water, she guided the girl into the bathtub.

The girl must have hated taking baths, because she scrunched up her face and grunted—but once Mutsumi shot her a glare, she straddled the edge of the bathtub, seemingly resigning herself to her fate. For a second, Masamune caught a glimpse of color through her bush, which made him tense up a little.

Mutsumi gently soaked a towel in the hot water, then gently scrubbed the girl numerous times, staring Masamune in the face as she did so. Then she handed him a different towel. She was asking him to do the same.

Masamune obligingly placed the towel on the girl's back. He didn't dare go straight to her arms or waist. He scrubbed the girl's soft body as carefully as he could. After all, the towel felt way too coarse…

By the time they left the steel factory, the sunset had already faded away.

The color of the sky felt like a reflection of Masamune's own state of mind. The vague, impassioned excitement he'd felt had well and truly faded.

"What are you sulking for?"

Masamune raised his head. He'd never helped anyone bathe before, let alone touched a girl's skin. He felt utterly drained.

"She really stank, didn't she?"

The girl's stench still felt like it was lingering in his nostrils. It was a stale aroma, and yet it wasn't especially unpleasant. In fact, it seemed like the kind of scent that would draw people in.

"She smells like that, no matter how much you wash her. I've never had a pet, but I guess that's what beasts are like."

Mutsumi kept on walking, waving her hand in front of her nose.

"Tuesday and Friday. Twice a week. I feed her, give her a bath…"

At that moment, a luxury Jaguar appeared from the direction of the steel factory parking lot. The steel factory's superstar, Mamoru Sagami, was in the passenger seat. The car passed them, heading toward town.

"He doesn't even look at me."

Mr. Sagami, with his characteristically intense gaze and hunched back, bore no resemblance to Mutsumi. It was hard to believe they were father and daughter.

"Does he make you do this?" Masamune asked, but Mutsumi ignored his question.

"You're not the type to find out a secret and run away, are you, Masamune?" she asked.

"…How come you're calling me by my first name all of a sudden?"

"You can call me by my first name, too."

At that point, Mutsumi came to a halt and peered into Masamune's eyes. Startled, Masamune flinched.

"Do you know how to write my name? You use the characters for *six sins. Mu-tsumi.*"

"Don't tell pointless lies. I'm pretty sure it has the characters for *harmonious* and *reality* in it."

"Hmm… You *have* been paying attention to me."

Masamune's face flushed red, but he gave up on trying to argue. He just wanted the ground to swallow him up.

Then Mutsumi whispered something to him.

"Remember how you called her a wolf girl?" she muttered. "Well, the real wolf girl is me."

"Huh?" said Masamune.

Mutsumi's mouth twisted into something resembling a smile.

"I'm the girl who cries wolf."

*

The only sound in the dark room was the rhythmic ticking of the owl-shaped wall clock's pendulum.

Masamune—who didn't even have the energy to switch on the lights—was drawing in his notebook, illuminated by the moonlight.

Nothing should have surprised him, no matter how weird it was. That was just the kind of world he was living in. And yet he'd been preoccupied by what had happened at the steel factory ever since he got home.

The girl, who'd looked a lot like Mutsumi Sagami, was shut inside one of the factory's blast furnaces. She was unable to speak properly, and there was something wolflike about her. Encountering her had shaken him up—but he'd also seen a girl his age naked for the first time. That was the *real* shock to the system.

His hands had been moving on autopilot. The warm steam had wavered in the soft sunlight that was shining through the window. He'd seen the girl's skin, which was as white as snow, beneath the surface of the water…

He thought about the day when the sky had split open. How many months and days had passed since the incident at the steel factory? Maybe Masamune was already at an age when it was normal to touch a woman's skin—an age when marriage could have been in the cards. Outside his window, however, it was permanently winter. Because of school schedules and work hours, counting the days of the week was permitted—but it was forbidden to count the actual months and days. Only the staff of the town hall's Citizen Affairs department were permitted to do so, and the relevant information was never disclosed.

There had been classmates who secretly counted the days, but they had disappeared from school without warning. *We saw that coming*, everyone had thought. They'd had a vague idea of what would happen. People doubted whether they would even be able to stay sane if they knew exactly how much time had passed.

Before he knew it, Masamune's hand—with which he'd been sketching the naked girl—was drawing in Mutsumi behind her. Mutsumi, who was wiping the girl's skin with a towel dipped in the bathwater, had a sad yet defiant look in her eyes. For a moment, Masamune felt like she was looking at him.

"Masamune!"

As soon as he heard his name, Masamune snapped back to reality. In a panic, he covered up what he was drawing.

His mother, Misato, who'd called out to him, was shouting from the bottom of the stairs.

"Take your grandpa, please! The disaster prevention meeting starts at eight!"

While his mother was yelling, Masamune crumpled the torn-out page of his notebook into a ball.

"Got it! Just give me a second!" he yelled back, tossing the paper into the trash can—but he quickly took it out again, feeling uncertain.

Then he tore the page into even smaller pieces. He needed to make sure nobody could deduce what the picture was of, even if they did happen to find the scraps.

"Masamune?!" Misato yelled, pressing him to come down.

"I'm coming!" he replied, still tearing up the paper.

When he went downstairs, he saw his grandfather, Souji, waiting in the entryway. He'd made it out of the living room, but he still seemed like a statue.

"Give me a second," Masamune said—speaking more to himself than anyone else—and then hurried outside.

Out in the cold night air, he unlocked the small car that was parked in the yard. After sliding into the driver's seat, he started the engine with practiced ease and opened the door.

"Get in," he called out to Souji, who'd joined him outside…

Masamune and his fellow townspeople were trapped in Mifuse—and so they were being forced to "remain unchanged."

This was to prepare for their return to their old world. If time began to pass normally again and people were different from how they'd been before, it might cause a whole other kind of distortion.

The town's policy insisted that people change as little as possible by making them fill out self-monitoring forms, preventing them from counting the days as much as possible, and encouraging them to maintain the same relationships.

However, some people questioned whether this was too unfair. Their arguments centered around the kids who'd ended up stuck in this world before reaching adulthood. They contended that if it was deemed that those individuals were already adults, they should be granted at least one "adult right"—as long as it didn't lead to any major changes in personal relationships, such as marriage or childbirth.

The Citizen Affairs department would send notices to each school—without specifying the exact duration of time passed—and children they deemed to have "reached adulthood" were then brought in to discuss their situation. There, they'd decide which adult privileges they'd get by majority rule.

Masamune drove the car down the highway.

"It's crazy that the only adult privilege I'm allowed is driving a car," he said.

"…You can't do anything in the countryside without a car," replied Souji.

"You can't do anything either way…"

The red traffic light seemed unusually dim that day. Masamune was a little late signaling, and a horn blared from the car behind them. When Masamune glanced in the rearview mirror, he saw that the driver was a child who looked even younger than Masamune—most likely a grade schooler.

The fact that even kids *that* age had received adult privileges made Masamune wonder how many years had passed—but he always pushed such thoughts aside so that he didn't get overwhelmed.

That day, though, the thoughts he usually managed to suppress were rudely intrusive. Maybe it was because of his encounter with that mysterious young girl.

What kind of rights had she been given?

There was a sign reading MIFUSE TOWN DISASTER PREVENTION MEETING at the entrance of the town hall.

A few town hall employees and factory workers were standing in front of the whiteboard inside the meeting room. Most of the attendees were elderly.

"Yes, my name is Jin Tachibana. Age…um, eighty? Or was it ninety?"

The elderly attendees, who were eating oranges, erupted with laughter.

"Hey, that's not good. Is he going senile?"

"That's a form of change. Arrest the guy!"

Masamune found his grandpa a seat with a view of the whiteboard, then walked toward the back of the room. Senba was there.

"I didn't know you'd be here," Masamune commented.

"Yep. They got me to bring the oranges," Senba replied.

The phrase *Fill in your self-monitoring forms regularly* was scrawled across the whiteboard. When Souji's turn came around, he rattled off his details in a monotonous tone.

"Name: Souji Kikuiri. Age: seventy-four. Spouse: none. Hobbies: none. Back pain: yes."

Among those who happened to be attending the meeting was a young woman. She was watching the speakers intently and would occasionally take notes. She appeared to be pregnant and had an empty stroller beside her. Whenever Masamune brought Souji to the meetings, she'd be there.

"All right, everyone. There's still a chance that we could return to our old world, so let's keep striving to avoid change…"

Masamune glanced briefly at Senba, then quietly left the meeting room.

The can of coffee fell out of the vending machine with a thud.

"Do you listen to the radio, Masamune?"

The sky was pitch-black, and the stars looked exceedingly bright. Masamune, who was in the town hall parking lot, pulled the tab to open his coffee. When he flicked it with his finger, it felt slightly sticky.

"Oh, that show where people write in? Nah. It gets on my nerves."

"I still listen to it from time to time," muttered Senba, narrowing his eyes a little. "You know how the DJ plays a song instead of answering the person's message? I kept listening to the songs he played, wondering what the meaning of them was…and it made me want to be a DJ, too."

Masamune could remember, as clear as day, the song that was on the radio at the time of the incident. It had played in his mind for a long time. After all, its title was "The Night When God Comes Down."

"I didn't think you'd be into that kind of job—one where you have to perform for people."

"Yeah. If we weren't in this situation, I doubt it would have ever been a dream of mine… I keep writing that I want to work at New Mifuse Steel Factory on my self-monitoring forms, though."

Senba had a high-pitched voice and was as sensitive as a girl, but Masamune always thought of him as manly. He seemed more thoughtful than their other classmates. He almost resembled Akimune in that sense.

Then Masamune heard the clattering of wheels…and the pregnant woman he'd seen earlier came out of the town hall's entrance. She'd put her shawl in the lower part of the stroller she was pushing. The pregnant woman kept her eyes glued to the ground as she walked away, refusing to look up.

"That's Mr. Yamazaki's wife. She was so pleased that she'd finally gotten pregnant, but the incident happened before she gave birth… The baby's still inside her belly."

The woman had been struggling to get pregnant for a long time. As the wife of the eldest son of a rural family, that alone had made her the target of criticism. Her mother-in-law would complain to neighbors about her—so much so that even kids like Senba heard the gossip. The woman was eventually able to conceive, but shortly before the baby was due… time came to a halt.

It had been so long that they weren't even permitted to keep track— and yet the woman was forced to carry on living with the baby inside her, only able to feel its heartbeat…

"I'm sure she'll get to meet her child once we make it out," Masamune found himself saying. He felt like he was going to scream with fear if he didn't say something.

He wasn't actually sure they would make it out, but he had to cling to that belief in order to survive.

"Yeah," said Senba with a small nod.

When Masamune looked up, he could see the silhouette of the steel factory looming in the darkness.

There was a young girl inside it. She didn't even have a name, she had to use a chamber pot, and she was given a bath on specific days.

Masamune might have been stuck in Mifuse…but that girl was even more trapped. So how…

"How can she smile like that…?"

"Huh?"

"Uhh, never mind."

Mutsumi Sagami had claimed to be a girl who cried wolf.

Masamune thought about the story. A young shepherd would lie to the people of his small village and shout, "There's a wolf!" He enjoyed watching the grown-ups scramble in fear. Eventually, though, they'd realized he was lying. Once everyone had stopped believing the boy's lies, a wolf *actually* showed up. "There's a wolf!" the boy cried, but nobody helped him.

And so the wolf ate the boy…

"……"

Masamune was dizzy. He'd just imagined the girl sinking her teeth into Mutsumi's slender neck.

Mutsumi's skin looked even paler than the other girl's, and it had red flowers scattered across it…

Masamune, who'd just brought Souji home, was thoroughly exhausted.

Unable to find the energy to take a bath, he walked past the open sliding door and stepped into his dark bedroom. Without turning on the lights, he placed his hand on the radio. He switched it on—hoping that particular radio show would be playing—but all he could hear was sleepy music.

Since they'd ended up in this world, no new programs had been aired on TV or radio. Instead, a few programs were played over and over again. For example, when Masamune's grandpa watched his usual detective series, it was usually the same episodes playing on loop. Each episode ended right before the culprit was revealed, leaving the identity of the criminal a mystery.

It was the same with commercials. Boring, familiar products were continually extolled as "brand-new."

Obviously, this was tedious and tiring…but people had no difficulty watching this stuff. For some reason, it never left much of an impression.

Masamune could remember seeing those things before, but nothing would truly sink in. It felt as though he had a thin film coating his brain.

Masamune picked up one of the manga magazines that was lying on the floor and threw himself onto his bed. There were never any new chapters, but he just kind of accepted it. In the past, he would have been desperate to find out what happened next, but he'd gradually stopped caring.

At the end of the day, everything was neither here nor there.

Then Masamune heard the roar of a motorbike engine. Tokimune had arrived.

Masamune absentmindedly recalled hearing that sound fade into the distance one day in the past. That memory was remarkably clear. Akimune, Masamune's father, had been reading this very manga magazine on the bed, just as Masamune was doing.

"Philosophical secret technique: Energeia?" his dad had exclaimed. "That's so cruel!"

A long time ago, Akimune had gone to a small, private university in the countryside—a rare achievement for somebody from Mifuse. There, he'd briefly dabbled in philosophy, even though it wasn't his major. It didn't seem like it came in handy in his current life, though.

"Energeia is a behavior unique to humans. It's all about living in the now, where actions align perfectly with their purpose and there's no gap between the beginning and the end… Still, the main character's behavior is actually very kinetic. You see…"

Whenever his dad started to ramble, it was usually because something was bothering him. Masamune, who'd come to this realization, inter-rupted his rant.

"You're skipping work again," he said in a mildly critical tone. "Uncle Tokimune came to fetch you and everything. How long are you going to stay away for?"

"It's not like I do anything there anyway. I've had enough of just *pre-tending* to work."

"You can't keep running away."

Masamune's harsh admonition brought a bitter smile to Akimune's face.

"Running away is what I've always done. I ran away from university and dropped out. I ran away from your mom…but she followed me to Mifuse—and we ended up having you."

"You make that sound like a bad thing."

"I don't regret that part. Being with your mom is easy, and you're an interesting kid. But…"

Akimune reached out for the fluorescent light, as though he was try-ing to grab hold of something.

"It's impossible now. I can't run away anymore…"

"But what about what that Mr. Sagami guy said? When the anger of the Sacred Machine subsides, things might go back to normal."

Akimune didn't reply. He just stayed lying down and opened the curtains a little. Seeing his side profile made Masamune feel a bit apprehensive—but like his dad said, he couldn't run away anymore. That provided Masamune with some comfort.

But when Akimune went out to work his first night shift in a long time, he didn't come home again.

*

The next day, when Masamune arrived at school, he found Sonobe by the entrance.

She was wearing her indoor shoes. Either Mutsumi had given them back to her or she'd found them herself. She'd been crying in the class-room the previous day, but from what Masamune could tell from her side profile…there were no observable changes. Her eyes weren't red from cry-ing her eyes out the night before.

"Did you get them back?"

"…! Uh…"

Masamune—unsure what else to say—automatically added, "Sagami was wearing your indoor shoes."

"…!"

At that, Sonobe finally turned around and glowered at Masamune. Despite her cutting expression and well-built physique, she seemed some-how frail.

"Don't tell anyone," she said.

"I won't. But are you sure you want to leave it at that?"

"I'm no match for Mutsumi, either way." Sonobe's head drooped a lit-tle, revealing a large mole on the nape of her neck. "Everybody likes her. Or maybe it'd be more accurate to say she's not disliked at all… Peo-ple aren't especially fond of her, but she's not hated on any level. I think there's a little animosity toward me, so everyone would side with her…"

"That's not true. *You* hate her."

"No…I don't hate her." Sonobe sounded hesitant, but you could tell she was trying her hardest to find the right words. "Still, when I'm with her…I feel kind of anxious. I don't really know why, but when I look at her…"

They heard footsteps hurrying toward them, as if in a deliberate attempt to interrupt Sonobe.

"Morning, Sonobe!" somebody said cheerily. It was Mutsumi.

Sonobe looked disappointed, but she quickly forced a casual smile and returned the greeting.

"Good morning."

Mutsumi glanced at Masamune, then turned away in a rather exag-gerated manner. With that, she and Sonobe walked away.

Mutsumi was keeping him at arm's length, making him almost doubt whether what had happened at the factory had happened at all. She was probably signaling that she intended for their relationship at school to remain unchanged.

Masamune felt like that was the most convenient scenario, too. If she kept dragging him around both during *and* after school, he wouldn't be able to handle it.

During lunch break, a conference was held concerning Sasakura's love life.

"It'd be a mess if the grown-ups found out, though, right?"

There were sections on the self-monitoring forms where they listed people they liked and people they disliked. Personal relationships were the area in which change was most strictly prohibited. Marriage, childbirth, and confessions of romantic interest were totally out of the question. Such events would cause too much incongruity if the townsfolk returned to their old world. Despite this, Sasakura was dangerously close to crossing the line.

"It's not like I want to date her or anything. I just want to have a little fun. You understand that, right?"

As Sasakura haltingly admitted what he'd been up to, Nitta and Senba made remarks like "Seriously?" and "Is that allowed?" There was so much excitement in their eyes, it almost looked as though they'd experienced the exhilaration firsthand.

This was understandable. What Sasakura had undergone was a form of change.

Still, to Masamune—who'd had an experience that had totally crushed his boredom—what Sasakura was doing seemed like no big deal. For the time being, though, the boys had decided to invite Mutsumi and the other girls to do karaoke together.

"Isn't karaoke kinda dull?"

"Where else are we supposed to go? Don't you dare suggest the library."

Masamune—who'd been letting the conversation go in one ear and out the other—looked up.

Mutsumi was standing on the roof. She wasn't lifting her skirt this time, but she gave him a slight nod. It was a much simpler gesture, and on some level, it felt reassuring.

"Where are you going?"

Masamune, who'd started to walk away, responded in a deliberately low voice.

"Somewhere bothersome," he said without turning around.

Sasakura and the others, having misunderstood his response, went "Oh, are you on duty today?" and waved him off.

Masamune didn't really want to lie to them, so he held his tongue.

"Here you go."

When Masamune made it up onto the roof, Mutsumi passed him a guide consisting of numerous sheets of paper. The phrase *Handling Instructions* was written on the front.

Masamune cautiously opened it to find the words *Twelve Things Not to Do* written on the first page, alongside rows of rules. These included *Don't touch her when not instructed*, *Don't talk to her*, *Make sure she eats all her vegetables*, and so on. All the text was written in neat and feminine handwriting, the small characters tightly crammed together.

"What is this…?" he asked. "Huh?!"

The rule that had just caught Masamune's eye made him cry out in disbelief. There it was, in black and white: *Don't think of her naked body when you masturbate.*

"Isn't that obvious?" stated Mutsumi.

"Uh… Sure, but… You can't write stuff like that! You're a girl!"

"What? If you argue back, I'll tell on you."

"And say what?"

"That you raped me."

After casually hurling this outrageous threat at Masamune, Mutsumi beamed at him. Her smile was gentle and sunny, unlike her words—and that made Masamune even more angry.

"…Who's going to believe a lie like that?"

"Everyone will. Yep. Everyone trusts me."

She was the girl who cried wolf. Masamune cursed her inside his head. *Eventually*, everyone stopped trusting the original boy who cried wolf—and yet...

"Why do I need to avoid talking to her?" he asked.

"She can't come out, so it'd be cruel to give her any false hope—don't you agree?"

Masamune didn't know why the notion of "false hope" had been brought up. It was absurd to talk about cruelty when Mutsumi was keeping her trapped in such a place, but he kept those thoughts to himself.

If he wasn't careful with his words, he would only end up being ridiculed once more.

They performed the ritual of bathing the girl at the steel factory, just like they had last time.

Masamune tried to keep his cool as much as possible, squinting to blur his vision as he wiped the girl's body with a towel. He couldn't afford to do this task without looking, though. If his hand accidentally touched her in a sensitive area, it'd be a huge problem.

After a while, the girl—who was compliantly allowing them to wash her body—turned toward the outdoors. Then they heard voices coming from outside the factory. Mutsumi stood up, shot Masamune a look urging him to carry on, and exited the room—leaving him and the girl alone together.

Only one person had left, and yet the room grew startlingly quiet. It wasn't as though there'd been any conversation before. Could one person's presence really make that much of an impact?

Masamune hesitantly continued scrubbing the girl's back, hoping to make some noise with the water, if nothing else.

"Your skin is so smooth," he found himself muttering, gently touching the indents of her shoulder blades with his fingers.

"So smooth," the girl repeated like a parrot.

The girl gazed intently at Masamune's lips, beaming. It looked like she was waiting for what he was going to say next. Just as Masamune was plucking up the courage to speak, Mutsumi came back.

"Never mind," he whispered, continuing with his work.

The girl immediately went quiet, staring at the floor several yards in front of her. Masamune considered asking Mutsumi a question as he was washing her back.

Isn't it much crueler not to talk to her?

Unsurprisingly, however, he didn't speak up. He simply continued to scrub her shoulders. That was the only part of her pale skin that had turned a little red…

Masamune wanted to talk to the girl. There was a lot he wanted to find out. Could he find a way to speak to her while Mutsumi wasn't looking…? He impatiently waited for their next visit to the steel factory.

When Friday finally came around, however, something unexpected happened. Mutsumi didn't come to school.

"Can someone take this printout to the Sagami household?" their teacher asked during homeroom at the end of the day.

Sasakura raised his head and glanced at Masamune. His face was practically glowing. Masamune understood what he was trying to say, but he wasn't sure what expression to respond with. At that moment, however, someone else volunteered.

"I'll take it."

Sonobe stood. It was typical for someone from the absent student's friend group to offer.

"Oh, thanks for that," the homeroom teacher replied, unfazed. He handed Sonobe the printout.

"Want me to come with you?" Sasakura suggested to her. "It's not like I'm busy today…"

He continued jabbering away, but nobody was listening.

"It's fine. I'll do it," Sonobe replied curtly, her expression somewhat stiff. She started walking away, her bag under her arm.

Sasakura snorted, then turned back to Masamune.

"Did you know? The less male attention a woman gets, the more they hang around cute girls. They think they might get some of her scraps," Sasakura claimed in a demeaning manner.

Masamune reflexively snapped back.

"That can't be true. I doubt it anyway."

Sonobe, who was making her way out of the classroom, showed some semblance of a reaction—but because she didn't stop in her tracks, Masamune didn't notice.

Mutsumi and Sonobe had stolen each other's shoes. Mutsumi claimed this behavior was fueled by boredom. Maybe the idea Masamune had come up with stemmed from boredom, too—but he saw her absence from school as a window of opportunity.

*

Masamune went home and got in the car. He had no grounds for entering the steel factory, but if someone did reproach him, he could simply say he was transporting goods. He'd be able to escape quickly, too.

Before making his way to the steel factory, Masamune headed to the rest area.

He wanted to give the wolf girl something a little warmer. After all, the place where she stayed seemed so cold. The first things that came to mind were the sandwiches he was so fond of. He covered the silver package that came out of the vending machine with his coat, hoping it'd stay hot for a bit longer.

Shortly after stepping inside the steel factory, Masamune made eye contact with a worker at the entrance—but the man walked away, showing no real reaction. He didn't seem to want anything, and he wasn't doing a very good job of patrolling the grounds, either. It really did feel like the steel factory ran itself.

Masamune stepped into the fifth blast furnace. There was a veritable sense of life inside the room, despite it being flooded with darkness. Masamune felt his way along the wall, a little nervous, then flicked a raised switch with his fingertips.

The room suddenly lit up. The girl, having already sensed Masamune's presence, was staring at him with her round, crystal-clear eyes.

"…! Oh…"

The girl's nose twitched as she realized Mutsumi wasn't present, and she seemed slightly suspicious. When Masamune flashed her an awkward smile, the girl smiled back.

There was nothing impure about her smile. Masamune was completely overcome by a sweet, ticklish feeling—the kind of sensation someone got when an animal took a liking to them.

"Oh… Um. Hello."

The girl was staring at Masamune, still grinning. As Masamune was dithering over what to do next, the girl got bored and started playing with her plushie.

She moved the plushie's arms around, gently tugging on them inside the cold concrete blast furnace. This sight alone had a tenderness to it, making the room feel like it had been brightened up by springtime sunshine.

Despite having braced himself for the situation, Masamune couldn't figure out what he should do. For the time being, he took the hot sandwich out of his coat. The girl's nose twitched again, and she came closer, crawling on her knees.

Masamune felt a subtle shift in his chest, but he spoke anyway, acting unfazed.

"Do…do you want this?"

"…Mm, want."

Though her pronunciation was unclear, the girl was able to catch what Masamune said and imitate it. Masamune hastily peeled back the foil and handed it to her.

The girl took a whiff of the somewhat warm sandwich and rubbed the surface of the bread with her fingers. She looked more like a pet cat than a wolf. She briefly licked the outside of it with her small tongue, and once she'd decided the sandwich was safe, she gently sank her teeth into it. She must have loved how it tasted, because she immediately took a big bite.

"Mm," she hummed, looking happy.

"This is what we call 'tasty.'"

"We call…ah, uhh…"

"Tasty."

"Chastee, ee."

It seemed she'd be able to talk normally if someone took the time to teach her. She simply wasn't used to speaking, as far as Masamune could tell.

"Hey… Who are you? You're not Mutsumi's twin or something, are you?"

The girl whipped her head up and said, "Mitsumi." She repeated the name again. "Mitsumi, Mitsumi."

"Um… Y-yeah. She's the girl who always comes to see you."

"Mitsumi, girl?" said the girl, continuing to repeat what Masamune was saying. It was unclear whether she understood or not. She appeared to enjoy saying *Mitsumi* and *girl*, though.

"Oh yeah. You need a name, too, right?"

Not giving her a name was cruel. When Masamune looked up, the number five—from the *fifth* blast furnace—caught his eye. Now that he was paying attention, he realized the number five was written all around the inside of the furnace.

"…Itsumi, maybe," he suggested. *Itsu* was one way of reading the number five in Japanese.

"Mitsu…Mitsumi, Mitsumi! Girl!"

The girl seemed to pronounce both the *mu* and the *i* sound as *mi*. No matter how many times she tried to repeat it, she kept saying *Mitsumi*.

"If you keep saying it like that, you'll end up having the same name as Mutsumi. We'll have to choose a different name for you…"

"Mitsumi!"

The girl whom Masamune had named Itsumi had gotten more and

more excited—and was now losing control. She boldly brought her face closer to Masamune's.

"Oh! And my name is Masamune…"

"Masamine! Girl!"

"I'm a boy."

"Masamine, boy! Mitsumi, girl, girl, Mitsumi!"

Itsumi ran around the room, getting pleasure out of uttering these words. She must have had plenty of stamina, because she kept jumping as she came and went. Itsumi flew past Masamune—who was dumbfounded—and started running deeper into the blast furnace.

"Heyyy… Uhh, Itsumi? Yeah, let's go with that. Heyyy?"

That was when Masamune, who had chased after Itsumi, came to a sudden realization. Behind the cluttered heap of materials, there were stairs leading out…

Once he'd come down the stairs, he found himself in a small, sunny courtyard. There were no workers in sight, and the vibe there felt sort of sacred.

There was a simple reason for that—the huge shrine archway that stood there. It was made from screwed-together steel, suggesting that it had been built out of materials from the steel factory—and it looked more like an art installation than an archway to a shrine.

Near the archway was a small freight train with a caboose attached to it.

Trees were growing around the train, and there was ivy wrapped around the train itself.

The juxtaposition of the rustic steel and the lush greenery had a unique beauty to it.

The train couldn't have been used in a long time. As Masamune walked up to it, Itsumi appeared on its roof.

"Hey, Mitsumi!" she said with a smile on her face. She was imitating the way Masamune had called out to her.

"Is…this your playground?"

"Ah-ha-ha!"

Itsumi grabbed hold of the train's railing and spun around it like it was a gymnastics bar.

"Watch out! Come on… Itsumi!"

"Mitsumi, watch out!" Itsumi repeated. She seemed to enjoy shouting.

She raised her hand toward the sun and gazed at the veins running through her palm. The smallest of things made her eyes sparkle with wonder. Her presence was so bright that Masamune seriously started to consider whether spending so long shut in the dark caused her to emit a light of her own—no matter how stupid that idea was.

Masamune stared at Itsumi in a daze. Then he suddenly put down his backpack and took out his pencil case and notebook. He enthusiastically pulled the cap off his pen with his mouth and began to draw… As he observed Itsumi in her natural environment, longing began to well up inside him.

At that moment, he heard the hysterical cry of a man coming from behind him.

"Hey, where are you?!"

Mr. Sagami had appeared out of nowhere, giving Masamune a shock. He wanted to call out for Itsumi, but it was too late. He ran behind the train and crouched down.

"Oh, ouch… Ugh, she's grown again. Whoa. Look at her. She's almost complete. A complete woman!"

Mr. Sagami was speaking excitedly to Tokimune, who'd come with him. He was in exceedingly high spirits, but not because he was pleased that Itsumi had grown. He appeared more interested in swaying Tokimune with friendly camaraderie. When Itsumi approached him, he shooed her away.

"Stay away," he said. "We don't want you falling in love with me, do we?"

Itsumi glanced at Masamune, who was hiding behind the train. Masamune shook his head frantically. Appearing to have taken the hint, she turned her head back around.

"Isn't Mutsumi around? I do hope that girl's doing her job properly."

The way Mr. Sagami referred to Mutsumi Sagami as "that girl" struck Masamune as extremely odd. After all, Mutsumi was his daughter.

"…Do you have any reason for keeping her here?" Tokimune asked.

"What? The Sacred Machine went through all sorts of trouble to summon her—the girl who shall become the god's wife!" Mr. Sagami gestured toward Itsumi, who was staring at him in confusion. He continued to speak, his voice shrill. "As long as she's around, there's a chance the Sacred Machine will pardon us! But—"

At that moment, Tokimune interrupted him.

"My brother told me a different story," he said.

This sudden mention of Akimune made Masamune tense up a little. Mr. Sagami glowered at Tokimune, disgusted.

"Akimune lost the ability to make accurate judgments. It's a shame, considering I was kind enough to make him my right-hand man…"

Then Mr. Sagami glanced at Tokimune out of the corner of his eye and made a blunt declaration.

"In this world, you're best off following my command… Please don't disappoint me, Tokimune."

Mr. Sagami was the first of the men to start walking away. Tokimune followed him with a bitter expression on his face—but as he did so, he chucked something toward Itsumi. It was a bag of snacks with KYABETSU TARO printed on it.

Itsumi enthusiastically accepted the gift and bit into the bag.

"…What was that about?" Masamune couldn't help but mutter to himself.

It was already pitch-black out by the time Masamune made his way home from the steel factory.

For the first time, he felt grateful that driving a car was the adult privilege he'd been granted. Too much had happened, and his thoughts were a mess. Being able to change the scenery around him with just a press of the accelerator was definitely something he appreciated. Everything kept moving, never coming to a halt.

As Masamune drove across the bridge, he spotted a familiar figure in a desolate area. He stopped the car and called out to them.

"Sonobe…?"

Sonobe, who had huge shoulders for a girl, turned around in surprise. She looked undeniably disgusted.

"What do you want? I said I would take her the printout."

"Printout?"

Masamune's confused reaction made the tension drain from Sonobe's shoulders.

"That is where Mutsumi lives…," she said. "But she wasn't there. She was playing hooky."

Mutsumi's house was at the back of the giant parking lot. Masamune only assumed it was a parking lot because there were cones positioned at unnecessarily large distances from one another to divide up the parking spaces. The lot itself was overgrown with weeds, and an abandoned scrap car had graffiti on its window.

Behind it stood what looked like a terraced house. That was where Mutsumi lived.

For some reason, Masamune felt shaken up. The shrine they ran might have been small, but the Sagami family was still a notable clan who had conducted Shinto rituals at the steel factory for generations. More than anything else, though, it was the vibes Mutsumi exuded that had convinced Masamune that they were extremely rich.

"Her dad isn't her biological father," Sonobe spat with a hint of spitefulness. She must have picked up on Masamune's reaction.

"You…," Masamune—who'd developed a dislike for Sonobe— muttered in a vaguely reproachful manner.

"The Sagami family wanted an heir."

The pair turned around, startled. Mutsumi was standing behind them, holding a bucket. She was dressed casually. Her skirt was much shorter than the one she wore at school, and she had black pantyhose on. Like with the house, Masamune had imagined her wearing something much more regal. Once again, he felt slightly taken aback.

"But that old geezer has no interest in women. The Sagami family picked out my mom, who was divorced with a kid in tow, but she died shortly after. And since there's no need for an heir in a world like this, they've thrown me out."

"…?! What are you talking about, Mutsumi…?" Masamune found himself shouting.

Sonobe's eyes widened, but she was shocked about something else entirely.

"Mutsumi?"

"Huh?"

"So you're on a first-name basis… I knew something was going on between you two."

"…! Something going on? Such as?!"

Sonobe strode away without saying a word. Mutsumi looked at Masamune in dismay.

"Oh dear."

"Is this my fault?!"

"You came in your car. Drive her home, won't you? You're the one who upset her."

Masamune wanted to stand his ground, but when he saw the contents of the bucket Mutsumi was holding, he dismissed the idea. Inside it was a stick of funeral incense, a lighter, and a rag. That explained why she'd taken the day off.

When Masamune returned to the car, he could see Sonobe walking off. Her pace was slow, and it seemed like she was waiting for Masamune to catch up with her.

He got into the car and started the engine. Sonobe flinched a little. He was unsure what to say, but when he slowly braked beside her, she came to a halt, too.

"So, uhh…do you want to get in?"

There was a sparkle in Sonobe's eyes. She gave him a slight nod, opened the passenger seat door, and clambered inside.

It was the first time Masamune had been alone in a car with a girl.

He felt awkward, so he put the radio on. *"But if I get into high school…,"* the DJ began. Of *course* that show where the DJ read out listener's letters happened to be on. He switched it off again.

They were still in range of the steel factory's glow, so the area was tinted orange. Sonobe gazed aimlessly out of the window and murmured, "I don't hate Mutsumi."

She squeezed her bag against her chest. "She…just makes me feel so hopelessly anxious."

Same here, Masamune thought.

✳

It was Sunday. Tokimune always turned up in the morning, parked his motorbike in the space in front of the porch, and carried out some maintenance with a cigarette in his mouth. He'd swung by from time to time when Akimune was still around, but from what Masamune could remember, he'd made an appearance only once every two months. The frequency of his visits had slowly increased, and he'd started showing up almost every week.

When he entered the kitchen, he found Misato whipping egg yolks and condensed milk into a froth. Perhaps she was going to make a cake. Baking was a hobby of hers, but neither Masamune nor Souji was particularly fond of sweet things, so she always baked something on a Sunday when Tokimune was coming.

"Baking's a great way to relieve some stress. As long as you measure your ingredients and follow the steps accurately, you can achieve the perfect result—like finding the answer to a math problem. That's what I like about it, the consistency."

In the past, Misato often made sweets for Akimune, who had a sweet tooth. After Akimune's disappearance, however, she didn't make anything for a while. It wasn't until Tokimune started coming around that she started baking again, using him as a taste tester.

Misato hummed a tune as she worked—a tune Masamune hadn't really heard before. As he watched her hands moving around, she poured what she'd made into a cup of coffee.

"Wait, is that it?"

"Yep. Here, take this to Tokimune."

Masamune placed the mysterious drink on a tray and carried it through the living room and onto the porch where Tokimune was tinkering with his bike. He was humming a tune, too. Then Masamune realized it was the same one Misato had been humming. Masamune wasn't sure whether this was a coincidence or if Tokimune had heard his mother and joined in, but both options made him slightly uncomfortable, bringing a slight frown to his face.

"Hey, Uncle Tokimune. Here's your tea."

He placed the tray on the porch, the cup still sitting on it.

"Thanks… Whoa, it's egg coffee!"

Tokimune stopped what he was doing and took a sip of the drink, looking pleased.

"That's so sweet! Oh yes, this is the stuff!"

Masamune was sure that Misato, who was still in the kitchen, would have heard his uncle's excited reaction.

"Our upperclassman got obsessed with it after traveling to Vietnam. He used to make it all the time when we visited his apartment."

Masamune understood that when Tokimune said *we*, he was talking about him and Misato. They'd attended the same university.

Tokimune had once—under the influence of alcohol—divulged that Misato met Akimune after coming to hang out in Tokimune's dorm, just as Akimune had stopped by to scrounge for food. Tokimune had played Cupid for the two of them, albeit unintentionally…

"This brings back some memories… It sure is sweet."

Tokimune's serene smile infuriated Masamune.

While the man enjoyed reminiscing about the past, he was also depriving Itsumi of the opportunity to create new memories. Tokimune might not have been the ringleader, but he was equally guilty. If the entire steel factory was complicit in keeping Itsumi trapped, who knew how many accomplices there were? He couldn't even trust his own mother.

Mifuse might have been teeming with boys who cried wolf.

"Uncle Tokimune, is it true that the fifth blast furnace…?"

"Hmm?"

Masamune almost asked about Itsumi but ended up faltering. That question was like Pandora's box. What if asking it made Itsumi's situation worse than it already was?

He could see that Tokimune was waiting for him to complete his question, so he decided to give his uncle a shock.

"Do you have your sights set on my mom?" he muttered quietly.

"*Pffffssshhh!*" went Tokimune, spitting out his coffee. This textbook display of astonishment brought Masamune a vague sense of relief.

*

After that, Mutsumi continued to wear her fake smile at school and pretended to ignore Masamune. That said, she'd still snort or give him cold looks if their eyes met while they were away from other students.

Strangely, Masamune interpreted this icy attitude as a sign of closeness.

During their regular visits to the steel factory on Tuesdays and Fridays, Masamune began to uncover unexpected sides of Mutsumi. At first, she seemed like a quiet person who was hiding a secret. Then she'd begun to show her mean and arrogant side. The more the two of them worked together, though, the more her assiduousness became apparent.

Despite making all kinds of rude comments about Itsumi's excrement and smell, she wasn't averse to dirty work. She meticulously took care of the laundry and cleaning. She'd clearly worked hard to take care of Itsumi before Masamune started helping her.

The same applied to food. Masamune had assumed she just bought any random stuff for Itsumi, but she had a firm grasp of what Itsumi liked, and she paid attention to the wolf girl's nutrition, too.

When she asked Masamune to help with Itsumi, it wasn't just to make things easier for herself. She genuinely needed an extra hand. When she requested his assistance, everything she said was truthful. Gradually, Masamune had begun to feel that Mutsumi might also be a victim.

Still, one thing struck him as odd. Mutsumi barely spoke to Itsumi. She claimed that it would be cruel to give her false hope, but the wolf girl didn't appear to want to talk to Mutsumi, either. Itsumi had such an innocent smile, but when she was with Mutsumi, her expression grew tense. Perhaps she sensed that Mutsumi was hard to deal with.

When Mutsumi was present, Itsumi would even act cold around Masamune. Although she seemed like a free spirit, Masamune had begun to suspect that she was more attuned to her surroundings than he'd thought.

Not only was Itsumi deprived of her freedom to do as she pleased, but her mental freedom was also being taken away. Anger had begun to well up inside Masamune. He was furious at Tokimune and Mr. Sagami, for example—but he struggled to feel particularly infuriated by Mutsumi. Seeing her in a vulnerable position made her easier to relate to.

Masamune still couldn't look directly at Itsumi while he was washing her. That said, he had gotten more used to the situation. He didn't go to the trouble of blurring his eyes like he had before, and he'd stopped awkwardly touching her.

He simply turned his face away and scrubbed Itsumi's body in silence. This inevitably led him to notice Mutsumi's shoulders, hands, and eyelashes from a slanted angle as she worked beside him.

As wavering steam rose from the bathtub, Masamune came to the intense realization that this girl named Mutsumi was delicate in every possible way.

In addition to his visits with Mutsumi, Masamune began secretly going to the steel factory by himself every Saturday after school. He'd get home from school, change into his everyday clothes, and then load his car with supplies. This particular day, he was taking her a picture book he'd read as a child, having taken it out of his closet.

If he left things for Itsumi at the steel factory, Mutsumi would find out what he'd been up to. He didn't know what punishment he might face for breaking the rules laid out in the "handling instructions." As a result, having a car was essential. It made it easy to bring items back and forth.

That day, when Masamune opened the door to the fifth blast furnace, Itsumi suddenly burst into tears and threw herself against his chest.

"Ahhhh, wahhhh!"

She wailed. It was as though she didn't know how to express the emotions welling up inside her.

"What's the matter? Oh."

Itsumi had opened her tightly clenched hand and showed something to Masamune.

In her palm was a crushed butterfly, the same one Masamune had seen before. Itsumi's fingers were covered in delicately shimmering scales.

"You tried to catch it, huh…? If you squeeze it too hard, it'll die."

"N-n-no… I no want it die…"

Itsumi's face was stained with tears. She seemed to understand the concept of death. Masamune gently patted her head.

"It's okay. Don't worry… It was probably already weak."

"Ugh… *Sniff.*"

"Butterflies don't survive in the winter anyway."

As Masamune said this, he was struck by a strange, unsettling sensation. Why had something that wasn't supposed to survive the winter been here at all? Could it really just be a coincidence?"

"Come on, take a look at this."

When Masamune passed Itsumi the picture book, she glanced up, still tearful.

Itsumi continued to sniffle for a while as they were reading the picture book, but she gradually cheered up and started stroking the illustrations with her fingers, exclaiming things like "Monster, a monster!"

She appeared to be able to read a little, as she was tracing the words intently with her eyes.

Masamune, who was sitting beside her, took out his sketchbook.

He'd always enjoyed drawing, but the more he fell in love with it, the more despondent he began to feel. The only time he genuinely enjoyed drawing—without being disturbed by any unwanted thoughts—was when he drew with Itsumi, a girl brimming with curiosity.

Suddenly, Itsumi sneezed. She must have been cold.

"That's strange," Masamune found himself muttering. He picked up a cardigan that had fallen on the floor.

In Mifuse, it was rare to see people sneezing because of the cold.

"Here, put this on… Wait, this is hand-knitted."

The thick yarn disguised it somewhat, but the cardigan was quite shoddily knitted. Several stitches had been skipped, and the yarn was uneven, but it was clear that someone had put in a lot of effort.

"Mitsumi give me," Itsumi said, her smile so reverent that she almost resembled the Virgin Mary.

"…I did think it looked pretty poorly made," Masamune remarked.

That seemed to annoy Itsumi. She snatched the cardigan out of Masamune's hands and hugged it tight. She seemed to treasure it more than the stuffed animal she always carried with her.

"I thought you hated Mutsumi Sagami. You don't say much when she's around…"

Itsumi said nothing, her face buried in the cardigan. Her silence seemed to answer Masamune's question.

It confused Masamune to discover that Itsumi liked Mutsumi, but somehow he also felt kind of happy about it. He was glad Mutsumi had displayed kindness in this abnormal situation, and that Itsumi, despite being trapped, truly accepted the compassion she was shown. Still, there was something Masamune wanted to know the answer to.

"Don't you want to get out of here?"

She seemed to have heard his question, but Itsumi didn't respond. Maybe she wasn't interested. Masamune looked up. Like light through a stained glass window, the sunlight that was streaming in gave their surroundings a celestial glow.

Masamune continued, even though he knew wouldn't get a reply.

"That said, it's not like you could get very far, even if you did get out…"

*

It was Friday, and it was cleaning time at school. Masamune was repeatedly mopping the same spot, wondering what to bring to Itsumi on Saturday. At that moment, Sasakura came over to him.

"It's decided. It's going to be tomorrow, Saturday!"

"Huh? What's decided?"

"We're gonna hang out with the girls. Obviously, you've got to invite Mutsumi Sagami."

Visiting Itsumi on Saturday had been the only thing on Masamune's mind, but Sasakura's imperious demeanor made him inquire further.

"What are we doing? Karaoke, wasn't it…?"

"The station, of course!" said Sasakura.

Masamune couldn't remember hearing anything about the station. He tensed up.

There was a station in Mifuse. It was a short distance away from the shopping district. Masamune hadn't been near it for a long time, though. None of his friends lived in that part of town, and most importantly, trains had stopped arriving after that fateful day. Since it wasn't connected to the outside world, he had no reason to venture toward the station.

That didn't apply to only Masamune. His classmates—including Sasakura—couldn't have had any reason for going there, either.

"Why the station…?"

"Isn't it obvious? There are ghosts there!"

Places seldom frequented by people often became breeding grounds for these kinds of rumors.

Shortly after a train left Mifuse, it would enter a small tunnel. There was an old rumor that a ghost of a woman—with only an upper body, long arms, and palms that were thirty centimeters in diameter—would tap on the windows while the train was in the tunnel. This rumor had been around since Masamune was a child. Still, why would people fear ghosts when things were already so bizarre?

"Crazy things happen when guys and girls are testing their courage. They scream. And then they cling to each other, you know?" said Sasakura, growing excited.

Masamune gave a nonchalant reply.

"Uh-huh."

"But do you think she'll come? That girl," Sasakura continued.

Masamune couldn't imagine Mutsumi coming along. Most girls were scaredy-cats, and Mutsumi tried to blend into that role at school. That said, the sight of the station at night probably wouldn't bother her.

"So whaddaya say?"

In the classroom after school, Sasakura's suggestion made the girls in Mutsumi's group exchange furtive glances.

"Come on, it'll be fun," Sasakura insisted, but Hara cut him down.

"Hanging out with boys at night? My parents would be furious," she said.

Yasumi was against the idea, too, stating that ghost hunting was childish.

"...Fine. I don't care about you guys anyway," Sasakura grumbled, annoyed.

"Hey, what did you just say?!" the girls retorted, sending him into a panic.

I guess we'll have to take a rain check, thought Masamune, who'd been listening to the exchange from close by. At that moment, however, Sonobe—who'd been quiet the entire time—muttered something loudly enough for everyone to hear.

"I guess I'll join you."

The girls' eyes widened, their attention turning toward Sonobe.

"You must be kidding, Sonobe. Why?"

"I thought you hated stuff like this."

As question after question was hurled her way, Sonobe kept her eyes fixed on one spot straight in front of her. It seemed like she'd already come to a decision. And then…

"Then I'll come, too," Mutsumi stated with a surprising degree of frankness.

While the girls—and even Sasakura—stood there with shocked looks on their faces, Mutsumi glanced at Masamune and flashed him a subtle smile.

"Sonobe's a good kid, isn't she?"

On their way home, Sasakura changed his long-held opinion of Sonobe.

It was already written in stone that Masamune would be joining, but he wasn't planning on pushing back. He always saw Itsumi alone on Saturdays… It sucked having that routine disrupted. There were picture books Masamune wanted to read to her and sweets he wanted to feed her. Still, it seemed like a bad idea to let Mutsumi—who'd flashed him that subtle smile—go without him.

She never usually smiled like that in front of the others, so why had she done it at that moment? Masamune had no idea.

*

They were supposed to meet up at seven, but Masamune arrived at Mifuse Station early. Maybe because he was nervous.

His surroundings were pitch-black. Every little breath and footstep seemed to be swallowed up by the darkness. There was a rusty chain blocking access to the station entrance—so Masamune stepped over it and went inside.

The inside of the station wasn't particularly dusty. Although it was devoid of life, it didn't feel like it had been abandoned for that long, either. The posters on the walls, which were torn at the edges, were advertising a small festival held when the spring wildflowers were in bloom. The flowers on display at the festival, which took place soon after winter ended, weren't particularly rare—but Masamune couldn't help but wonder if Itsumi had ever seen them. As he was pondering these kinds of questions, Sasakura, Nitta, and Senba turned up. About twenty minutes after they'd arranged to meet, Mutsumi and Sonobe appeared, putting on an air of importance.

"I'm so sorry we're late."

"Agh," Sasakura gasped. His face went red, and he tugged gently on Masamune's clothes.

"Hey, is that what Mutsumi Sagami usually wears?" he asked. "They're shorts."

Mutsumi and Sonobe were clinging to each other, linking arms. At first glance, it looked like they were just acting like close friends—but Sonobe's expression was gloomy, as though Mutsumi was restraining her.

Masamune and his classmates jumped off the platform and onto the tracks.

The railroad, which had dark trees looming behind it, only extended a short distance before plunging into the mountain. The tunnel was small—only about one hundred meters long—and designed to receive outgoing trains. If Sasakura was correct, this was where crazy things happened between guys and girls.

"Rock-paper-scissors! Whoever throws the same symbol pairs up!"

They'd decided to split into pairs for the test of courage. Masamune and his classmates, who'd already decided on their partners in advance, pretended to play rock-paper-scissors a few times without coming to a draw. As this was going on, Sasakura unsurprisingly got Mutsumi to stand close to him. At that moment, he shouted in a hackneyed manner, "Agh, this is a pain to think about. Let's just pair up the girls and boys on either side!"

No one objected, so Sasakura delightedly partnered with Mutsumi.

Nitta was with Yasumi, Senba with Hara, and Masamune with Sonobe.

"We've got this," Sonobe said to Masamune in an inexplicably defiant manner.

"The rules are simple!"

The rules for the test of courage, as explained by Sasakura, were straightforward.

They were to go to the middle of the tunnel and graffiti something on the wall to prove they were there. It could be a picture, a message, anything.

Sasakura and Mutsumi were the first to head into the tunnel.

As the others waited on the moonlit platform, the cool, damp sensation of the asphalt seeped up from the ground they were sitting on.

"They're taking forever."

"Maybe Sasakura's jumping on Mutsumi Sagami."

While the others chatted, Sonobe stood stock-still. She was wearing a beige pinafore that was about the same length as her school uniform skirt. The poor-quality fabric was wrinkled around the butt area, and her thick legs were covered in red pores. It seemed like everything in the world was cruel to Sonobe.

After a while, Sasakura and Mutsumi came back.

"Hey. We're done," announced Sasakura, sounding somewhat arrogant. His face, meanwhile, was stiff. "It's your turn next, Masamune."

Masamune glanced at Sonobe, who replied with a slight nod.

Masamune stepped into the tunnel alongside Sonobe. Their footsteps echoed loudly in the chilly air. The flashlight he was carrying illuminated only a small area around them.

"Are you okay?" he asked Sonobe. His voice sounded as if it were coming from someone else, reverberating noisily around the tunnel. It was somewhat eerie.

"Yeah," Sonobe responded, her reply soft and indifferent. After that, she stayed quiet.

He wanted to get the awkward silence over with as quickly as he could, so Masamune picked up his pace. According to the rumors the grown-ups had spread, the tunnel was blocked by debris partway through, preventing anyone from going any farther. Masamune shone his flashlight at the wall, hoping they'd gone far enough. There, he saw some familiar handwriting.

"Oh, this is what Sasakura and Mutsumi wrote…"

The graffiti read *Sasakura was here*. That was definitely the kind of message Sasakura would leave. Underneath it was the name *Sagami*, written in shaky-looking script.

"I guess we should write something here, too," Masamune suggested, spray can at the ready.

Sonobe, who was beside him, reached out her hand.

"I'll write first," she declared.

Intimidated by her indomitable attitude, Masamune handed over the spray can. Sonobe shook it vigorously a few times.

"It's not coming out properly…," she said, beginning to draw some kind of symbol on the wall.

At first, Masamune watched absentmindedly—but once he realized what was happening, he became startled. She was drawing a simple picture of an umbrella with a heart on top.

Sonobe wasn't finished yet. Under the umbrella, she added two names.

Masamune + Yuuko

"…! Wh-what's that? Who's Yuuko?"

"…That's my name."

Come to think of it, he vaguely remembered that being the name written on the inside of Sonobe's indoor shoes. Sonobe looked directly at him, her eyelids puffy and her pupils constricted.

"Do you know what this means?" she asked.

Unsure how to respond, Masamune started rubbing his own name with his hand, acting on impulse. The spray paint wouldn't come off, but the action made Sonobe jolt with surprise.

"…Do you hate me?"

"N-no. Never mind that, though. Do you…?"

"I think I like you."

"Then why did you…?"

"I think I like you, Kikuiri. You gave me a ride in your car."

Masamune had been in a state of confusion, but the ludicrousness of Sonobe's response caught him off guard. Without realizing it, he raised his voice.

"Th-th-that's not how liking someone works, is it?!"

How *did* liking someone work? Masamune didn't have an answer. Sonobe continued, undeterred.

"Do you like anyone, Kikuiri?"

"Huh…"

Itsumi's face came to mind, but he doubted he liked her in the way Sonobe was envisioning… As Masamune wavered, the image in his head evolved into Mutsumi.

"I knew you liked Mutsumi," she stated. It seemed as though Sonobe had read his mind.

"…!"

Masamune felt his ears warm up. At that moment, what sounded like deep breathing—*hoo, hahhh*—echoed through the tunnel. It felt as though the stagnant, cold air of the tunnel was being stirred around by the person's breath.

"What was that sound?"

A voice echoed from the darkness. Masamune quickly directed his flashlight in the direction of the noise.

"You idiot, Sasakura! Ssshhh!"

Sasakura and the others stood a short distance away. Mutsumi was there, too. The expression on her face was tense and confused—a far cry from the act she usually put on in the classroom.

"H-hey. Sorry. There was just this weird noise, right?" Masamune began.

"Yeah, we didn't mean to startle you. I just thought we should stick together…"

We came to see what you were up to…"

Sasakura and Yasumi mumbled glib excuses.

The mood was awkward. Sonobe glanced not at Masamune but at Mutsumi, shooting her a defiant look. Mutsumi stared back, her gaze steady and devoid of any discernible emotion.

"…!"

Without warning, tears started pouring from Sonobe's eyes. Seemingly unable to contain her emotions, she shoved past Sasakura and ran out of the tunnel.

"Wait, Sonobe!" Masamune called.

Everybody ran after her in a panic. Masamune hesitated, glancing at Mutsumi. The look in her eyes was slightly reproachful, prompting him to follow the others.

Once Masamune burst out of the tunnel, his surroundings seemed weirdly bright. He presumed this was because he'd just come out of the darkness, but he soon realized he was mistaken. Giant fissures had opened in the sky, and green light was pouring out of them.

The sound of deep breathing continued echoing around them.

"This is just like the day of the incident…," Senba muttered.

Sonobe, who was running in front of him, came to a halt. She looked up at the sky above the railroad. The light flooding out of the cracks was creating spots at her feet.

"Sonobe!!" Masamune called out, his eyes opening wide with shock.

Sonobe was emitting green light, from her neck right down to her back. It wasn't that the light from the fissures was shining on her. This light was beaming straight out of Sonobe.

"Mutsumi. You and I were messing around to distract ourselves from our boredom, weren't we…?" she said. "We were trying to suppress our desire to run away."

Sonobe's broad shoulders were shaking. The panting sound was resonating from Sonobe, too—albeit to a lesser extent. Then the light slowly began to spread.

"Right now, I…feel so embarrassed I just want to run away."

Sonobe slowly turned around, looking in Masamune's direction.

Her face was dappled with green spots. The light stretching out from the base of her neck had reached her cheeks. With tears in her eyes, the edges of her lips lifted into a slight smile. Then Masamune heard a subtle cracking sound, like that of plastic breaking. A single hole opened on the front of her neck. And then—

"I said how I felt, and it turned me into a laughingstock."

As soon as she'd uttered those words, cracks started forming in Sonobe's skin. The cracks—which were centered around the hole in her throat—made an unpleasant snapping noise as they spread. It was just like *that* night.

Stunned and unable to move, Masamune and the others watched as something bizarre happened behind Sonobe. This time, it wasn't in the sky, but at the factory.

"Smoke?!"

The smoke the steel factory continually puffed out suddenly billowed up larger than ever, assuming the form of a pack of wolves. They were all joined together at the base, making them look like a multiheaded serpent.

The pack of wolves began to dart around the night sky. Some of the wolves raced toward the cracks in the sky and used their own bodies to fill them up. Then one of the wolves came plummeting toward Masamune and his classmates at breakneck speed.

"Whoa!"

As Masamune and his friends crouched down, the smoke wolf skimmed just above their heads. As they tried frantically to prevent the wind pressure from knocking them off their feet, they heard a loud, panicked cry.

"…! Sonobe!"

It was Mutsumi. She usually never lost her composure. Masamune looked up.

Sonobe was standing frozen in place, staring at the smoke wolf hurtling in her direction. Mutsumi began running toward her. Masamune followed, but the wind pressure caused him to stumble and fall.

"Get down, Sonobe!!"

Mutsumi dashed fearlessly toward the other girl, but when she was just a few meters away, she was overtaken by the smoke wolf plunging toward her classmate.

"Ahhhhhh!!"

It looked as though it was going to devour her—but just then, the light from the cracks in Sonobe's body broke up into particles, flashing violently before dispersing into a mist.

"Sonobeeeee!"

The light subsided—and Sonobe was gone.

There was no sign of the wolf, either. It was hard to assess what had even happened. The fissures in the sky had closed completely. With no moonlight, Masamune's surroundings were pitch-black—and Masamune was struck by the illusion that he had somehow been transported back into the tunnel without realizing it.

Everything seemed the same as before…apart from the fact that Sonobe had disappeared, leaving her clothes and shoes scattered on the ground.

"Oh… W-we need an adult! We need to call an adult!"

"…! Y-yeah."

Everyone else had finally regained their composure and begun to run around, but Masamune couldn't bring himself to move a muscle. Sonobe's obstinate, stubborn-sounding words kept ringing in his ears.

"I think I like you, Kikuiri."

*

"What the heck is happenin', Mr. Sagami?!"

"They're saying she was devoured by a wolf made of smoke?!"

The grown-ups who'd gathered at the town hall in the middle of the night were clamorously laying into Sagami. The guys from the factory—who were standing on either side of Sagami at the long table in front of the whiteboard—were looking glum. Tokimune was one of them.

Mamoru Sagami himself, meanwhile, looked fairly calm.

"Hey. You realize their friend was *eaten*, right? You've gotta give us some more info!" someone shouted. This made Masamune and his classmates, who were huddled in a corner of the meeting room, shrink back in alarm.

"Stop it. I'm sure those kids are in shock as well…"

Hara was usually so feisty, but the ruckus the adults were causing had brought her to tears. Masamune could do nothing but stare blankly around the room. But then…

"Chomp!" Mr. Sagami suddenly shouted. Everyone's attention turned to him. "Did the wolf really eat her? Like that? With its mouth open?"

Sasakura and the others exchanged glances.

"W-well, it looked like it vanished the moment they collided…"

"Exactly!" exclaimed Mr. Sagami, seeming pleased with himself. He picked up a marker and began writing energetically on the whiteboard. "Did you see the sky tonight, everybody? There were large cracks in it, weren't there? There were tons of cracks in the sky on the day the factory exploded, too. And then the smoke from the Sacred Machine—"

The marker squeaked as Mr. Sagami finished writing the final letter. He then recited what he'd written on the whiteboard in large print.

"The Sacred Wolves sealed up those cracks!" The words *Sacred Wolves* were written in huge writing. When he saw the stir he'd created in the room, Mr. Sagami smiled contentedly and continued speaking. "And… they did the same with the cracks in that schoolgirl's heart."

"…! The cracks…in her heart…"

"Maybe something happened that created fissures in her heart. That's why the Sacred Wolves tried to seal them up…"

Masamune felt like his own heart was being crushed.

The wolves had come to fill the cracks in Sonobe's heart—but rather than having those fissures sealed up, she'd vanished… No. Perhaps the quickest way to erase the cracks in someone's heart was to obliterate the person themselves.

"Ah, hey. Masamune!"

Masamune had dashed out of the meeting room. He couldn't bear to listen to any more. Undeterred, Mr. Sagami looked around at his audience and let out a cry of satisfaction.

"We're all in this together. We're all here in this same world, experiencing the same pain. For that precise reason, we must *never* entertain the idea of escaping!"

The dark shopping street was completely deserted, and the only movement was the shuttered storefronts trembling slightly in the night breeze. Masamune was sitting on the cold curb.

In the unobstructed rural winter, he could hear police car sirens in the distance. Then came a monotonous announcement.

"A large amount of smoke is being produced. Please return home immediately and secure your doors…"

A horn blared, breaking the silence with a sudden burst of noise. Masamune weakly lifted his gaze, only to be met with the headlights of Tokimune's motorcycle.

"What are you doing, Masamune?"

"…! Uncle Tokimune…"

Tokimune got off his bike and took Masamune by the arm, trying to bring him to his feet.

"Hurry up and go home. Your friends have already gone—"

"No!" Masamune shouted.

He shook off Tokimune's hand.

"Why do I have to shut myself away at home? I'm already trapped in Mifuse!"

"Calm down, Masamune."

"No! I don't want to stay here! I want to be in a big city with bookstores and movie theaters! I want to do tons of studying and see all sorts of new things… I want to become an illustrator!"

"Come on, it'll be fine."

"What will be fine?!" Masamune glared at Tokimune with tears in his eyes. "I can't trust you! You knew about Itsumi!"

"Who's Itsumi…? Oh."

The look on Masamune's face was enough to tell Tokimune who he was talking about.

"How could you do that?! Dad must have known, too! Were you two okay with locking her up in a place like that?!" Shaken by what had happened to Sonobe, Masamune couldn't contain the storm of emotions he'd been holding back for weeks—emotions that had been brewing since their world had changed. "Why won't you answer me? Cat got your tongue?"

Tokimune looked anguished as he accepted his nephew's tearful plea.

"That girl doesn't belong here," he muttered.

"…! What…?"

"Just come with me."

Tokimune tried to put a helmet on Masamune. Masamune resisted slightly but eventually gave in. Tokimune patted Masamune on the head.

"I'm going to protect you on behalf of my brother," he announced. "I'll protect you…all of you."

"I'm not asking for that," murmured Masamune, feeling somewhat frustrated.

Once Tokimune had brought Masamune home, Misato only asked if he wanted a bath and didn't press for more details. She'd probably heard the rumors already.

Masamune, weighed down by a sludge-like fatigue, climbed the stairs and entered his bedroom. He sat down on his chair, not bothering to turn on the light. That was when he spotted the self-monitoring form lying on his desk.

When he switched on the reading lamp, the *People I Like* and *People I Dislike* boxes came into view.

Upon seeing these sections, Masamune was overcome by a bizarre scorching sensation. He wanted to cry and scream at the same time. He grabbed a mechanical pencil and started writing in a frenzy.

For the first time, a girl told Masamune Kikuiri that she liked him.

Tears blurred his vision, making it difficult to see if he was writing clearly. Nonetheless, he continued to scrawl frantically across the page.

But that girl disappeared. Because of me. Because there was another girl. Because I liked another girl.

"…!"

Masamune used his pencil to furiously scribble over the word *liked*. He applied so much pressure that he tore his self-monitoring form. The lead broke. Still, he kept scratching and scratching…and a voiceless scream escaped his lips. He pounded the desk, then slammed his face down on it.

Sonobe is gone.

Because…I liked that other girl.

*

By the start of the following week, Sonobe's desk had vanished from the classroom. The teacher had put it away.

During break, Sasakura and his friends started playing a mah-jongg card game. They laughed out loud as they hid their thin mah-jongg tile cards from one another. It was as if the "test of courage" night had never even happened. But that wasn't all. It felt as though the fainting game they'd played to distract themselves from their boredom—as well as the conversations they had about girls, most of all Mutsumi—had been forgotten.

Even Hara and Yasumi, who'd been totally drained by the ordeal, were now chatting normally. If anyone looked close enough, though, they would see the redness under the girls' eyes. It was obvious they'd been crying all weekend.

Masamune had no idea what state Mutsumi was in. He couldn't even bring himself to look at her. He didn't want their eyes to meet, he didn't want her to read his emotions…and more important than anything else, he was inexplicably terrified.

Masamune didn't go home after parting ways with Sasakura after school that day. Instead, he went straight to the steel factory.

Having crossed the bridge, he looked at the roadside shrubbery. That was the spot where the wildflowers from the poster in the train station would bloom in the spring. Would it make Itsumi happy if he brought those flowers to her…? They'd never blossom in this incessant winter, but he entertained the idea nonetheless.

"Masamine!"

The moment he opened the door to the fifth blast furnace, Itsumi hugged him.

"Whoa…?!"

She must have been waiting impatiently for him, having heard his footsteps approaching. She was like a loyal dog waiting for its master to return. She looked up at him with a beaming smile on her face, her small hands clinging tightly around his waist. She seemed determined to never let go.

The moment he saw Itsumi like that—

Masamune collapsed to his knees.

"Ugh… guh, ugh…"

Tears poured ceaselessly down his face.

Was he grief-stricken over Sonobe's disappearance, crushed by guilt, or horrified by the abnormality of the situation he'd found himself in? Masamune wasn't sure, but he couldn't stop crying.

"Masamine? Masamine?"

Itsumi called out his name, sounding concerned—but her feeble, delicate voice just made him cry even harder.

"I…I'm sorry. I…I—I…" Then Masamune felt something cold gently touch his nose. "Huh?"

He looked up. Itsumi was leaning over him. This force caused Masamune to tumble backward, and Itsumi landed on his stomach with a thud. She kept pressing her nose against his nose, his mouth, and his chin, like a dog or cat greeting a companion.

Their lips ended up brushing against each other slightly, but it definitely wasn't something anyone would call a kiss.

Still, every time Itsumi's lips touched him, something slowly spread throughout his chest. This sensation was soft and incredibly warm—just like Itsumi's lips.

"Itsumi… Do you know what it means to like someone?"

"Like?"

Masamune's spontaneous question garnered nothing but a puzzled look from Itsumi.

Masamune wondered what Sonobe had meant when she'd told him she liked him.

She claimed she liked him because he drove her home, but that wasn't how it worked. In that desolate tunnel, she'd started to cry, saying that she'd become a laughingstock. That wasn't what liking someone was. Masamune knew that, but still…

"But…I'm strange, too."

As he felt Itsumi's weight pressing against him, Masamune thought of Mutsumi.

Liking someone was supposed to be gentle and kind. When a person liked someone, they tenderly exchanged their warmth with them, like he was doing now…or so he thought. However…

"For me…this isn't what it means to like someone."

A certain girl's face came to mind, the image of her crystal clear. That girl—Mutsumi Sagami—looked just like the one who was right in front him, sharing her warmth when he was hurt.

"When I like someone, it feels a lot like hating them…and it kinda hurts. I know it shouldn't be like that, but…"

Just then, a loud crashing noise came from behind, interrupting Masamune's tearful speech.

"…?!"

Masamune's heart pounded fiercely. He didn't want to turn around, but he had no choice. Resigning himself to his fate, he looked behind him…to find Mutsumi glaring at him, just as he'd expected.

Still, there was one aspect of the situation that he hadn't foreseen. Mutsumi's face was bright red.

"What do you think you're doing?!" she yelled. It was rare for her to show her emotions so openly, and she was speaking in a spiteful tone she wouldn't normally use.

"M-Mutsumi… It's not what you think. Itsumi was…"

Masamune's voice cracked. Mutsumi ignored Itsumi, who seemed apprehensive, and stormed straight over to Masamune. Once he was within reach, she grabbed him by the collar.

"I guess you are a scummy guy after all!"

"Ouch. Let go of me!"

"Who's Itsumi anyway? Don't tell me you gave her a name?!"

That was when Masamune realized he had referred to Itsumi by name—and made peace with the fact that he was in a hopeless situation. Scolding someone for referring to a person by their name wasn't a normal thing to do.

"That's right! She's committed only five sins, as opposed to the six you claim to have in your name. That's why she's Itsumi!"

Masamune pushed Mutsumi away with a forceful shove.

"Gyah?!"

Mutsumi was much lighter than he'd expected, and she toppled onto the floor. *Crap*, he thought, but it was too late to regret what he'd done. Still pumped full of adrenaline, he yelled out to Itsumi.

"Come on, Itsumi! I'll get you out of here!"

"Out of here…?"

"Just come! I'm gonna show you all sorts of stuff!"

Masamune yanked hard on Itsumi's arm. Mutsumi was still on the floor, showing no sign of moving. When Masamune glanced at her…he was left stunned.

"What? Why are you crying…?"

"…! Huh…?"

Tears were streaming down Mutsumi's cheeks. She hurriedly wiped them away with the back of her hand. Maybe she hadn't even realized she was crying. Then someone shouted at them, asking the same question Mutsumi had posed just moments earlier.

"What do you think you're doing?!"

When Masamune looked up, he saw Mr. Sagami and Tokimune standing at the entrance of the fifth blast furnace.

"Masamune… You…"

"This way, Masamune!"

Mutsumi called out to him and started running. Masamune hesitated for a moment, then took Itsumi by the hand and followed the other girl's lead. The adults yelled at them as they ran away.

"Where are you going, Masamune?!"

"You're willing to defy a god?! You insolent fool!"

*

Masamune ran, Mutsumi taking the lead. At first, he was pulling Itsumi by the hand, but she eventually started running on her own. Thanks to her beast-like speed, Masamune ended up being the one chasing after her.

They'd bolted out of the fifth blast furnace, but the tall, rusty structures of the steel factory and the dense clouds overhead made it feel like they'd never be able to escape, no matter how far they ran. Even so, running was Masamune's only option.

Eventually, they reached the outskirts of the steel factory. There, they found a seemingly discarded freight train and an abandoned platform. It didn't appear to be in use. With its boom still up in the air, the motionless mobile crane looked like a giant sculpture.

"Why is there a train at the fifth blast furnace when there's a platform right here?"

"That's because—," Mutsumi began, but before she had the chance to finish her sentence, the sound of breathing started to echo through the air. Itsumi looked up at the sky joyfully and joined in.

"Hoo-hah, hoo-hah!"

Masamune felt sick. It was the same sound they'd heard during their test of courage. Back then, the sound had come from the sky—as well as Sonobe…

"Wahhh?!"

A low rumbling noise—like the sound of an earthquake—interrupted Masamune's thoughts. The ground beneath his feet was trembling. Ferocious clouds of dust were swirling up from the rocky surface of the iron mountain behind the steel factory. It seemed like the rock face had crumbled slightly.

When Masamune looked up at the sky, he found countless cracks in it, just as he'd expected.

"But something…feels strange."

As the breathing sound went on, the cracks in the sky continued to stretch out and release light. This warm light seemed to be bulging out of them.

When he strained his eyes, he could see what looked like color behind the cracks. As cloudy as the sky was, there was a dazzling gleam that was captivating yet aggressive at the same time.

"Aha!"

Itsumi let out a cry of delight and started climbing the crane that led to the roof of the platform—as if to get closer to the sky. Masamune, who'd been in a daze, snapped straight back to reality.

"Stop that, Itsumi. It's danger—"

His voice cut off.

Itsumi stretched out her narrow limbs as she scaled the ladderlike crane. It was hard for her to grip the rusted shaft with her small hands, and her feet slipped, preventing her from making much progress. Despite this, she kept climbing, as if giving up was never an option. Her eyes gleamed like the light that could be seen through the cracks. She was simply enjoying herself, targeting her prey…and seemingly trying to escape to the outside world.

"Yeah… I guess danger doesn't mean anything there."

Masamune also wanted to see what was behind the cracks. He *wished* he could see it.

He began climbing the crane, following Itsumi's lead. He didn't know what lay ahead, but he wanted to cast aside the current version of himself—the one that had adapted to the uncertain world and refused to change.

Mutsumi didn't follow Itsumi and Masamune, but she didn't try to stop them, either. She simply stared, entranced, into the cracks.

At that moment, a loud siren interrupted the quiet excitement. Tokimune and Mr. Sagami had caught up with them. "Masamune!" they shouted.

Mr. Sagami was panting heavily, his shoulders heaving. He didn't seem used to exercising.

"Now give us back that girl!"

Mutsumi stepped in front of the crane, blocking the two men.

"No way!"

"What? Mu-Mutsumi?!"

Mutsumi's firm refusal left Mr. Sagami flustered, allowing Tokimune to step forward.

"Masamune! Listen to me. Don't move…"

"No way!" Masamune shouted, just like Mutsumi had. "Why shouldn't I move?! I want to see it, too! I want to see so much more!"

"See more, more, more," Itsumi murmured excitedly. She was reacting to Masamune's statement.

Itsumi kept climbing, reaching for the cracks she could see above her. Unable to contain his fear, Mr. Sagami shook his head and shrieked.

"No! Come back… Stop that!"

Tokimune gulped, nervous and full of anticipation.

"Maybe…if she touches it…"

Masamune realized he was getting caught up in Itsumi's excitement, but he couldn't stop himself. He didn't want to, either. If only he and Itsumi could keep running—

"Ahh. I want to see more. A whole lot more."

"More, more, more, more!!"

"More, more, more!"

"Mooooooore!!"

The light from the cracks—wafted along by the north wind—slowly moved to the area above Itsumi's and Masamune's heads. Mr. Sagami yelled desperately.

"Ah…!!"

The light from the cracks soon swallowed up Masamune and Itsumi entirely. At that moment…

Chirrrrrrrrrr!!

Masamune heard the absurdly loud chirping of cicadas. This sound, which he hadn't heard in so long, assaulted his eardrums.

The cloudy sky had vanished, replaced by sunlight so dazzling that it made his surroundings look white. He couldn't open his eyes fully…but when he strained them—

"…! What…?!"

This wasn't the steel factory he knew. The positions of the buildings and the mountains in the distance looked the same, but most of the factory's structures were destroyed, out of use, and in ruins.

Despite this, there seemed to be more life around than before. Vines were crawling over the buildings like they were creatures, plants had sprouted everywhere, and the intense sunlight was reflecting off the dense greenery.

It was a summer scene, plundered from a distant past.

*   *   *

As the steel factory teemed with palpable vivacity, Masamune raised his hand to block the overwhelming glare. Immediately, though, another shock hit him.

His palm was letting all the light pass through it—and it wasn't just his hand.

"I-I'm…see-through?"

The outline of Masamune's body was rapidly beginning to blur in the summer sunlight. As the summer light appeared to vaporize everything into whiteness, he was gripped by the terror that he, too, might evaporate.

And yet Itsumi's silhouette stood out sharply against the backlight. Without thinking, Masamune clung to Itsumi's waist. He felt like he was going to disappear right there, right then. He didn't understand why, but he was convinced of it. He closed his eyes, as if resigning himself to his fate—but then suddenly…

"…Huh?"

A cold north wind, completely inconsistent with summer sunlight, started blowing from below. The strong wind made the cracks shift again, passing over the top of Masamune and Itsumi. The two of them had been brought back to the winter world—or rather, they'd been ousted from the summer.

"Masamune, Itsumi!" called out Mutsumi, who'd been waiting for them in the winter.

Once the cracks had fully gone by overhead, the pair reappeared. Masamune's body, which had turned transparent, gradually returned to normal.

Mr. Sagami's face was scrunched up as if he was about to cry. He let out a laugh that didn't match his expression at all.

"Ha-ha… Ha-ha-ha! You must be kidding! Even *that* girl can't escape through the cracks. What a surprise!"

Mr. Sagami lifted his hand in an exaggerated motion. Smoke began to surge from all over the steel factory, as if his gesture had been a signal. The smoke soared into the sky, forming the shape of wolves.

"Oh Sacred Wolves! Seal up the wounds of this world!"

The Sacred Wolves began to fill the fissures in the sky. Once the shattered sky was fully restored, they gently dissipated.

"Uncle Tokimune! What was that view we saw beyond the rifts…?" Masamune asked reproachfully.

"…That was reality," Tokimune reluctantly replied.

It took Masamune a moment to grasp what he was saying.

Reality was a common word, and yet it felt so foreign—as if he were hearing someone say it in a different language.

Flustered, Mr. Sagami grabbed Tokimune by the arm.

"H-hold on, Tokimune. I thought we agreed to keep that a secret from everyone…"

"We can't keep hiding it," said Tokimune, dismissing Mr. Sagami's panic. He continued looking Masamune square in the face. "We've been imprisoned in Mifuse as a punishment. The idea that we might one day escape…was a lie to prevent you all from losing hope."

"A lie?!"

Masamune instinctively glanced at the "girl who cried wolf," but Mutsumi stayed silent, her sidelong expression as icy as ever.

✳

"Sure, it was a lie, but only a minor one," Mr. Sagami insisted.

He was standing on the platform in the town hall parking lot, showing no remorse to the citizens who'd gathered there. Snowflakes were gently falling around him.

"To be precise, this world is an illusory space created by the Sacred Machine…but that doesn't make much of a difference…"

"It's a *huge* difference!" Hara was the first to interrupt Mr. Sagami's speech. "If this isn't reality, what even are we?!"

Hara's rebuttal led the other onlookers, who'd been watching Mr. Sagami's proclamation with meek expressions on their faces, to start a chorus of commotion.

"What do you mean by *illusory?*"

"Is this the afterlife?"

"Does that mean we're dead?"

"Are we ghosts?"

"If this world was 'created,' then that means it's a sham."

"Both Mifuse and its people are fake, then. I'm fine with that."

It seemed some of workers at the steel factory—like Tokimune—knew the truth, while others didn't. Some were confronted individually and could only respond with bewilderment.

"Why did you keep this secret for all this time?! Explain, right now!"

As angry shouts filled the air, Mr. Sagami appeared to be regaining more and more of his composure.

"If this world isn't real, what's the issue?" The unexpected response made the crowed flinch for a moment. Mr. Sagami opened his arms out wide and spoke in a pretentious tone. "Has it caused you any inconvenience until now? As long as no cracks appear in your heart, there's no problem with it. This world is an illusion—no, a fleeting mirage—and thanks to that, we can live forever!"

"I don't want that kind of eternity!" Senba had been the one to shout over the bustling crowd. Masamune looked around in shock, exchanging glances with Sasakura and his other classmates. Senba was usually so quiet. "I don't want this! I don't want to be trapped in Mifuse forever… unable to grow up! I refuse!"

The veins on Senba's forehead bulged as he screamed, leaving everyone speechless. As a weighty silence filled the parking lot, the sound of Sagami clapping once echoed through the air.

"All right. Have you finished ranting now, little boy?"

"What are you…?!"

"The most important thing is that this world carries on forever. To ensure that, we must give this girl back to the Sacred Machine!"

As he said this, Mr. Sagami glanced at Itsumi. She was standing behind Mutsumi, curiously looking around. When the grown-ups realized who he was looking at, they started whispering to each other, saying things like "I did hear rumors about her" and "So she's the god's woman…"

"…! How is he still claiming that…?!" said Masamune, about to step forward—but Tokimune gently restrained him with his hand.

"Let's put an end to this, Mr. Sagami," said Masamune's uncle.

"Huh? Tokimune?"

"The cracks have been increasing year by year, even when she's shut away. No matter how many times the Sacred Wolves repair them—"

Tokimune looked around at the crowd, then made an emphatic declaration.

"The end of this world isn't far off."

The restless crowd fell silent—but it took only a moment for them to start murmuring again.

"…The end?"

"What does he mean by *the end*?"

"The end, as in…"

"This fabricated world is going to disappear."

"Disappear… End…"

Their whispers grew, spreading like ripples and quietly pervading their surroundings.

"Wh-what are you talking about, Tokimune…?"

"We obeyed you because we were so apprehensive, so clueless about this world… But answer me this, everybody. Do we need rules in a world that's about to end?"

Upon hearing Tokimune's question, the people began to exchange glances. The tension that had been hanging in the air moments earlier started to change.

Everybody already knew that Tokimune was right—even if only on a subconscious level.

All Tokimune had done was put it into words.

"Th-that's a good point."

"If it's ending anyway, I guess we don't need to listen to Mr. Sagami…"

"What?!" exclaimed Mr. Sagami, looking around restlessly. "Hold on a moment. Are you out of your minds?"

Once the penny dropped, things moved quickly. People started talking freely among themselves, ignoring Mr. Sagami.

"Let's just go home, then."

"Might as well do whatever we want now."

"Hey, let's hurry up and eat that crab in the fridge before it goes to waste."

"W-w-wah… Whoaaaaaa!" Sagami screamed, climbing down from the platform and pointing at people's faces one by one. "This is crazy! Whoa! Are you people nuts?! What's wrong with you? You're on a totally different wavelength!"

"Mr. Sagami," began Tokimune, trying to pacify him—but Mr. Sagami was too shaken to stop yelling.

"Don't you care about what happens to this world?! Am I the only sane one left?"

At that moment, Mutsumi stepped in front of Mr. Sagami, her expression icy cold.

"Cut it out, old man."

"Y-you…!"

Sagami turned to Mutsumi and raised his hand, but she wasn't intimidated in the slightest. Instead, she lifted her fist to threaten him, causing him to cower away.

"Hyah?!" yelped Mr. Sagami.

"Whether this world is an illusion or not, it's about time you faced reality," Mutsumi said firmly.

"Ugh… Aaaargh!"

Masamune gently placed his hand on Itsumi's shoulder. She'd been watching the ordeal in puzzlement. Her shoulders were really small, but they felt far from weak.

*   *   *

"Kya-ha-ha-ha!"

Itsumi's excited laughter was engulfed by the unfathomable darkness of the night sea. As she ran around, Mutsumi chased after her, exasperated.

"Hey, sit still!"

Masamune and his classmates were sitting on the seawall, waiting for the bus. The group of girls, which included Hara and Yasumi, were at the covered bus stop—but Mutsumi seemed too busy with Itsumi to join them.

"She sure is energetic," Sasakura remarked, sounding like an old man. Then, in a weary tone, he added, "Mutsumi has surprised me, though."

"She has?"

"Yeah. She's more like a professional wrestler than a TV presenter. One from a hostile stable, like the Atrocious Alliance."

Regardless of how weird the situation was, Sasakura still managed to make a boorish remark.

Nitta responded with a nonchalant "Yeah, yeah," then turned to Masamune. "You saw reality, didn't you? What was it like?"

"Yeah. It looked like stuff was in ruins."

"Oh, that's because of the accident at the factory…that day."

This world was created on the day of the explosion. It was the last day they'd spent studying for their high school entrance exams—a pursuit that was now pointless.

"If the factory is gone, Mifuse's finished."

Most of the people born in Mifuse got a job at the steel factory and worked there until they retired. Without it, there would be almost no way of making a living in the town.

Senba, who'd been quietly listening, suddenly muttered, still looking down:

"*Mifuse* is finished?"

A heavy silence fell over the group. They were sitting on the seawall they used to jump off for fun. In fact, they were sitting right on its highest point. They always tried to leap from the highest, most dangerous part of it.

That's right. When Masamune and his friends were playing games, they opted for the ones that would hurt the most. The fainting game was one example of that.

That wasn't just to distract themselves from their boredom, though. They did it because pain was something they scarcely experienced.

For that precise reason, they longed for pain.

And not just pain, either. It was the same with the cold. In their world of perpetual winter, they'd still forget to turn on the *kotatsu* or space heater. There was no need to.

There was one thing the people of Mifuse had all noticed, albeit on a subconscious level.

They were all illusory beings.

"Come on. At this point, what have you got to lose by telling him how you feel?"

Over at the bus shelter, Hara drooped her head dejectedly as Yasumi patted her enthusiastically on the back.

"But…it's not that simple," argued Hara.

"You said it'd be awkward if you ended up at the same high school, but that's not a possibility anymore, is it?"

Yasumi's reasoning left Hara at a loss for words.

"Ugh…"

Yasumi smiled mischievously.

"You love him, don't you?"

Hara, whose entire face had gone red, fidgeted restlessly with her thumb and ring finger.

"I—I do. But still…"

"It hurts?"

This sudden interruption made Yasumi and Hara look up in astonishment. Itsumi had unexpectedly poked her head around the bus shelter. Flustered, Mutsumi compensated for her mischief by saying "Sorry, Haraaa! Itsumi's leaving now!" and pulling her by the hand—but Itsumi shook her head and refused, staying put.

"Love…hurts?"

For some reason, this question—which was directed at Hara—gave Mutsumi a shock. She looked at Itsumi, stunned. Hara didn't know what to say, either, but she seemed determined to continue nonetheless.

"Yeah, it does. Not in a bad way, though… It's a sweet pain."

Hara's earnest statement made Yasumi burst out laughing.

"Ah, ah-ha-ha! I can't believe you're making me laugh at a time like this!"

"Wh-what's so funny?"

"Sweet?" echoed Itsumi.

"She's trying to say that it's *bittersweet*! She likes the pain! What a masochist. Ha-ha-ha!"

"Shut up, or I'll silence you forever!"

"Gyahhh!"

Itsumi watched the two girls chatter away with a vacant look in her eyes. For a moment, Mutsumi—whose face was turned to the side—looked bitter.

*

At school the next day, the self-monitoring forms the students had submitted were given back to them.

"When your name is called out, come up and fetch your form. Ueda… Kaneko…"

When the teacher called out their names, the students walked to the front to collect their forms. Their homeroom teacher had compiled and stored their forms in separate files. The students had handed in these forms on countless occasions, so the binders were quite thick.

"What's the use in getting these forms back now?" said one of the students, as they chatted among themselves. "Should we just burn them?"

Meanwhile, the teacher glanced at Masamune and called his name.

"Kikuiri."

"…! Yes…"

Masamune walked up to the teacher's desk, feeling a little hesitant. The teacher handed him a binder with nothing more than his name on the cover. There were no self-monitoring forms inside.

"You managed to get away without submitting a single one, huh?" said the teacher.

"…Sorry," Masamune replied.

His teacher chuckled softly and looked out the window.

"Maybe you had it right all along."

Outside the window, a Sacred Wolf was gliding leisurely through the white sky…

Since the people of Mifuse found out that their world was an illusion, they started seeing Sacred Wolves almost every time they looked up at the sky. The steel factory continuously belched out smoke, which would then take the shape of wolves. These Sacred Wolves drifted around the winter sky, seeking out cracks, biting into them, and transforming to seal them up.

The Sacred Wolves came into being because rifts appeared—in the sky, and in people's hearts.

When a Sacred Wolf sniffed out one of these cracks, it'd soar right over to them. Driven purely by instinct, they'd attempt to fill the gaps.

One time, a middle-aged man was fishing by the sea. As he stared intently at the water, struggling to catch anything, he was consumed by a Sacred Wolf and disappeared. In the pocket of the fishing vest that he left behind was a photograph of his grandchild, who lived far away.

Another time, a mother was waiting at a traffic light with her child. She was holding her child's hand with a worried expression on her face when she was consumed by a Sacred Wolf and vanished. Her child was too shocked to cry.

* * *

Another time, a boy was running a marathon in gym class. He was a lap behind everyone else. He'd never been fast, but that day, he was distracted. He appeared to be moving his legs on autopilot, absentmindedly gazing at the sky above.

Then Masamune overtook him from behind.

"What's up, Senba? You don't look so good."

"I want to feel something real," he said. Senba's breathing was totally unlabored, despite the fact that he was jogging.

"Huh?" went Masamune, unable to grasp what his friend meant. He glanced at the space in front of Senba. There, a Sacred Wolf was floating elegantly before him.

"They're around all the time lately, aren't they?" remarked Masamune. "Swirling around in circles without a purpose…"

"We're the ones who are lacking a purpose," said Senba, his voice unusually cold. He was normally so composed.

Once again, Masamune shifted his gaze away from the sky and looked at Senba instead. As soon as he did, he broke out in a cold sweat. From his chest to his neck, Senba was emitting light. Slight cracks had appeared on his skin. It was exactly the same as what they'd witnessed on the night of the test of courage.

"We go around in circles inside Mifuse—circling the town without a purpose. There's nowhere else we can go, and there's no purpose to our lives. We simply keep going 'round and 'round…"

"…! Senba…"

Senba's eyes were becoming unfocused. The fissures on his chest started to split, making cracking noises.

That very next moment, a loud roar erupted. A ferocious wind rushed down from above, threatening to crush Masamune and Senba. Dust was swept up into the air—as if it had become weightless.

"Kyaaaah!"

The shrill shriek of a female student made Masamune look up. The blinding dust storm made it hard for him to open his eyes, but he could still see a Sacred Wolf diving straight toward them.

Everyone threw themselves to the ground in panic, but Senba remained standing, gazing up at the sky. Then the dust blocked everything from sight.

"Senbaaa!"

By the time the dust settled, both the Sacred Wolf and Senba were gone.

The students started raising their voices, shouting, "No way."

"S-Senba's gone!"

"Seriously?!"

At that moment, the gym teacher hurried over and blew his whistle.

"Hey! Don't look! Your hearts will crack!"

Masamune stood there in a daze, unable to speak. His eyes were fixed on the only thing left behind—Senba's gym clothes.

It was a slow suicide.

After school, Masamune and the others walked down the deserted highway, not saying a word. The fallow fields were full of withered plants. Masamune had forgotten what things looked like in the summer and couldn't tell what had once been planted there.

Usually, Masamune, Nitta, Sasakura, and Senba would have walked home together—but that day, it was just three of them. Only one person was missing, but for some reason, things looked so different.

After a while, Sasakura spoke up, his voice hushed.

"Senba's dad has the exact same eyebrows as him."

Senba's parents had been at the school gate earlier that day. They were there to collect his belongings, including the gym clothes he'd left behind when he disappeared. Both husband and wife had a diminutive build, just like their son. Senba's mother had been crying, but she didn't blame the teachers for her son's strange disappearance.

In Mifuse, nothing was abnormal.

Under ordinary circumstances, the disappearance of a friend would have come as more of a shock. In truth, though, nobody was supposed to be in this world to begin with. Senba's motive for vanishing would catch up with everyone eventually.

Masamune and his friends weren't sure whether they should be surprised or sad. All they were left with was a sense of helplessness.

"There's no reason for any of us to disappear...," Sasakura muttered in frustration. Masamune wanted to say, *This world is going to end soon regardless*, but he stopped himself. Instead, he contributed to the conversation in a different way.

"...The thing is, Senba had a dream."

"A dream, huh?"

"Dammit... I can't take this anymore. Everything's just so shitty..."

"Stop it. If you keep on like that, a wolf will come for you."

Sacred Wolves patrolled the sky, ready to pounce at the first sign of a crack in somebody's heart. The three classmates walked on in silence, aware that their hearts could easily fracture if they continued to express their feelings.

After parting ways with Sasakura and Nitta, Masamune headed to Mutsumi's house.

Since bringing Itsumi home from the fifth blast furnace, Mutsumi had started skipping school more frequently. There were still some things they both had to get used to, and their lives were undergoing significant change.

Masamune didn't feel like being alone that day—likely because of what had happened to Senba. He wanted to see Itsumi's face. He knew nobody could hear his inner thoughts, but he made a declaration inside his mind.

—It's Itsumi I want to see. Not Mutsumi.

As he approached Mutsumi's home, Masamune spotted someone who looked like Mutsumi doing some sort of work in front of the house. With her back toward him, Mutsumi was using a steel wool pad to scrub some marks off the wall. These stains hadn't been there the other day. When Masamune squinted to make out what they were, his face flushed with anger.

"What the heck is this?!"

Profanities had been scrawled across the wall with black spray paint.

This is your fault.

Bitch.

Pest.

"Some people think Itsumi's the reason the world is ending."

"Huh?!"

"Mr. Sagami made a big fuss, claiming it was because the god's woman had escaped."

"That bastard!" Masamune shouted, flying into a rage—but Mutsumi remained calm.

"None of us actually know the truth. It is what it is."

"That doesn't mean it's okay to attack Itsumi…"

"Masamine!"

The door beside the kitchen suddenly swung open, with Itsumi peeking out.

"No! Stay inside!"

Flustered, Mutsumi tried to stop her, but Itsumi pouted, deliberately slamming the door open and shut.

"Hey!" Mutsumi shouted again. Itsumi ignored her. She conveyed her anger however she liked, and she rebelled however she wanted, too. The two of them seemed to have gotten a lot closer.

Masamune looked back at the graffiti on the wall. The word *demon* was scrawled across it. The contrast between the playful scene in front of him and the hateful graffiti on the wall was too extreme.

After a moment of thought, Masamune made a suggestion—albeit a little nervously.

"If you want to…," he began.

Dinner at the Kikuiri household looked completely different that evening.

Souji hadn't moved from his usual chair, and Misato was laying out yet another unremarkable meal on the *kotatsu* table. And yet one thing was out of the ordinary: Mutsumi and Itsumi were there.

"Are you sure that's okay…?"

"Of course. I'll watch Itsumi while you're at school."

Itsumi ate with her hands, her eyes sparkling at the sight of the meal before her.

"Please use a spoon… Hey, stop!"

Itsumi stole some simmered meat and potatoes from Masamune's plate. She stuffed her cheeks full of food, then opened her eyes wide.

"So sweet… Me like."

This simple reaction brought a smile to Misato's face.

"Oh, that's lovely to hear. Eat as much as you want," she said.

Itsumi, however, stopped there.

"…It no hurt, though," she said softly.

At that moment, they heard a motorbike engine.

"Oh, Tokimune's here," exclaimed Misato, looking up.

The mention of Tokimune's arrival made Mutsumi look a little nervous, but Masamune gently reassured her.

"It'll be fine," he said.

As it happened, all Tokimune said when he discovered that Itsumi was there was "Oh, right." It didn't seem like Itsumi had any particular feelings toward Tokimune, and she calmly carried on eating with her hands—producing a steady stream of "Stop! Stop!" from Mutsumi.

"I'm heading home," announced Tokimune.

Whenever he came on his motorbike, he'd spend the night by the *kotatsu*—but this time, he simply had a light meal and then stood up again. He didn't even drink anything. He must have felt awkward staying.

After walking him to the entrance, Masamune took the opportunity to ask how Mr. Sagami was doing.

"Well, he hasn't come to the steel factory. I've heard he's been spending time with his cronies and getting up to something shady…" Tokimune sighed and looked directly at Masamune. "Look after that girl, won't you?"

Mutsumi and Itsumi were staying in Misato's room, which was separated from Masamune's room only by a retractable curtain. It used to be Misato and Akimune's room, so it was bigger than the guest room. Misato, meanwhile, was sleeping in the guest room.

Masamune felt unsettled. When the girls went to take a bath, he retreated to his room to draw—but the possibility that they might see his artwork came to mind, so he hastily tidied up.

When Masamune went downstairs to make coffee, Itsumi came running out of the bathroom. Her hair was still wet, and she was wearing his sweat suit.

"Masamine!" she called out.

When Masamune looked up, he saw Mutsumi standing there, too. She'd also just gotten out of the bath.

"We were given the chance to take a bath first," she explained.

She was wearing Misato's pajamas and had a towel wrapped around her wet hair, revealing the nape of her neck. Masamune's heart skipped a beat, and he hastily averted his gaze. When he noticed that Itsumi was watching him, seemingly amused, he made a comment to distract her.

"Oh, that's my sweat suit," he said. "It looks nice on you."

"…Heh-heh."

Itsumi smiled, rubbing her cheek against the clothes. She looked adorable, but not in her usual innocent way.

"……"

When she saw how Itsumi was acting, a sour expression appeared on Mutsumi's face—but Masamune didn't notice. He was still struggling to meet her gaze.

*   *   *

It was the middle of the night. As the hum of the refrigerator reverberated around the dark kitchen, Masamune filled a glass with water and chugged it. The sounds of laughter and occasional rustling from the adjacent room had made him restless, and he wasn't able to sleep. His throat was parched.

"…Hahhh."

The living room was unusually bright. The moonlight must have been pouring in through the window. When Masamune glanced into the living room, however, he felt a shiver run down his skin.

There was someone in there.

He gulped, albeit gently. He made his way toward the living room, trying not to make a noise. That was when he finally realized: It wasn't the moonlight that was shining, but the cracks that had formed in the night sky.

Somebody was sitting on the veranda, illuminated by the flickering light. It looked like a man.

"It's done, Mutsumi."

"…?!"

The man who was sitting on the veranda looked at Masamune.

The middle-aged man seemed familiar to Masamune, as if he'd seen him before. *He looks like my dad*, Masamune thought.

The middle-aged man had stuck some disposable chopsticks into an eggplant and was holding what was now shaped like a horse.

"Is Grandpa going to come back riding one of these? That's kind of cute," he muttered.

Masamune, who was standing there in a daze, thought he felt someone walk by him. When he turned to look, a woman holding a newspaper appeared in the light.

"Oh…"

Masamune couldn't help but let out an exclamation of surprise. The middle-aged woman he was looking at resembled Mutsumi.

"The evening paper arrived."

"Oh, thanks."

The man took the newspaper from the woman and casually opened it.

When he saw the flyer inside, he flinched. He hurriedly tried to close the paper, but the woman reached over and grabbed the flyer before he had the chance.

"May I?" she asked.

It was a flyer for the *Obon* festival fireworks display. Cheerful slogans like *Free pork miso soup* and *A nostalgia-inspiring cargo train from New Mifuse Steel Factory works will be in operation!* featured alongside exciting photos and drawings.

"They said there might not be fireworks at the Obon festival this year...," the woman murmured quietly—but the calmness of her voice seemed to be stifling strong emotions.

"Yeah, but this will probably be the last time," said the man.

"...Yes, that's true."

The woman's expression grew more serene and detached, her face turned to the side.

"I'll make some coffee," said the man, looking apologetic.

"Oh... Oh..."

The man who looked a little like Akimune walked toward Masamune. He had a mole in the exact same spot on his neck as Masamune.

Then who was the woman who looked like Mutsumi...?

Masamune tried to step forward to get a closer look, but then—

"Watch out!"

Mutsumi suddenly grabbed Masamune from behind and pulled him toward her. The sheer force of this action caused them both to tumble onto the tatami mat in the living room.

At that moment, there was a powerful gust of wind. When Masamune looked up, he noticed that the Sacred Wolves had arrived.

The Sacred Wolves began to seal the cracks in the sky. The room soon grew dark as the middle-aged couple quickly faded away.

"I didn't realize we could see the real world when we were indoors...," said Masamune, glancing at Mutsumi with an expression of disbelief. "Wait, why aren't you surprised?"

"I *am* surprised. Maybe the light from the cracks was reflected into the house…"

"No, that's not the issue here!"

As Mutsumi came to terms with Masamune's bewilderment, she let out a small sigh. Then she began to tell the story of the first time she met Itsumi.

"There was a name tag…on the backpack she was wearing."

"Name tag?" Masamune repeated.

Mutsumi nodded gently.

"It said Saki Kikuiri."

Masamune's heart thumped loudly.

"…! So that means she's our…"

"She's not *my* kid," Mutsumi snapped, refusing to let Masamune finish his sentence.

"…! B-but…that woman was you, wasn't she?!"

"That's the *real* me. She's totally different from the 'me' who's here right now."

"Ugh… B-but you even act like Itsumi's mom at dinner."

"If I was her mother, I wouldn't shut her away like that. I'd never let her suffer year after year," said Mutsumi, sounding as though she was chastising herself. Then she sighed. "I'm sure that person is a kind mother, though…waiting endlessly for her missing daughter to come back. It's not like there's any way of sending Itsumi back to reality, though."

The living room—which had been filled with the light of summer just moments ago—was now enveloped in the chilly cold of a winter night. For some reason, though, Masamune could feel the dynamism of life all around him.

Itsumi was his daughter from the real world.

She was the only thing that was real in this world of illusion.

Maybe that's why she was called the god's woman and imprisoned in the fifth blast furnace.

And the older version of himself—who'd been perched on the veranda in the summertime—had Mutsumi, Itsumi's mother and his wife, by his side.

Mutsumi was Masamune's wife.

*

There was gentle snowfall at school the next day. In the courtyard during a break, Hara called Nitta over. Hara, who was blushing, kept her gaze down.

"Oh, right… I never would've guessed."

"I wasn't planning on saying anything, either! But…I'm not afraid of anything anymore. I wanted to know how you feel, Nitta."

Nitta replied to Hara's nervous confession frankly.

"I wouldn't mind going out with you," he said.

"…?! D-does that mean…you like me, too?"

"Well…maybe a little?"

Nitta was trying to play it cool, but his ears were bright red. Tears of joy welled up in Hara's eyes. Suddenly, a loud, off-key whistle echoed through the air. When the startled pair looked up, they saw their friends leaning out of a window in the school building.

"Go on, kiss her!"

"Congrats, Hara!"

Sasakura and Yasumi were looking down from a hallway window, encouraging and teasing them from above. Ever since Senba had disappeared, there'd been a somber mood hanging in the air. It'd been a long time since such cheerful cries had rung out.

Masamune smiled vaguely and glanced at Mutsumi, but she seemed to be deliberately avoiding his gaze. There was no chance of them making eye contact.

*

After school, after Masamune and Mutsumi had said good-bye to their respective friends, they met up in a vacant lot full of piles of scrap wood along the highway to the steel factory.

It was a secret that Mutsumi and Itsumi were living at Masamune's house, so they decided to meet outside of school.

Masamune, having arrived first, felt nervous—as though they were a couple having a rendezvous. Maybe witnessing Hara's confession had affected him.

Mutsumi was taking her time. The snow was really coming down, but Masamune didn't feel cold.

Eventually, Mutsumi showed up. She didn't seem like she was in much of a hurry.

"Did I keep you waiting?" she asked.

"Not really," Masamune responded curtly.

Masamune had asked Itsumi what she wanted to eat before leaving the house that morning. "The shiny bread," she'd said. He figured that when she said *shiny*, she was referring to the silver aluminum foil. She must have wanted one of the hot sandwiches from the rest area he'd once brought her. When Mutsumi caught wind of this, she looked at Masamune reproachfully and said, "I can't believe you've been feeding her in secret."

Masamune promised to buy a hot sandwich for Itsumi after school, and Mutsumi decided to come along.

"I should have brought an umbrella," Mutsumi remarked as the road began to turn white. Their surroundings had taken on the hues of a black-and-white ink wash painting.

"Let's just get inside for now," Masamune said.

The two of them dashed through the falling snow and into the rest area.

There was nobody inside, likely due to the weather. The lights—which, for some reason, had red and blue cellophane over them—did a poor job of illuminating the room.

The pair shook the snow off their clothes and hair like dogs shaking off water. Though they weren't particularly cold, being wet was uncomfortable, so Masamune turned on the heater.

When he switched on the massive heater, it started to hum and let out the vague smell of kerosene—at least, it seemed that way. In this world, even the smells were indistinct.

Itsumi was the only one who emitted a strong scent. Maybe that was because she was real. Thinking about that made Masamune's chest sting.

"I turned on the heater," Masamune said, turning around.

Mutsumi was casually perched on a tall stool, wringing out her wet skirt. Her slender calves were on full display, illuminated by the strangely colored lights—making the scene look oddly sensual. Masamune hurriedly averted his gaze and looked out the window, from which he could see the distant sky.

The sky was filled with a pack of Sacred Wolves, which were now a familiar sight.

"I can't believe people actually confess their feelings. I've never seen it happen before."

"What do you mean?" Mutsumi asked.

"I always saw Hara as tough, but she looked so feeble... She was shaking."

"Hara's a romantic. On her self-monitoring form, she put 'marrying someone she loves' as her future dream."

"What did you write?"

"A preschool teacher."

"Why lie about something so insignificant?"

"Well, it's better than being stubborn and refusing to write anything at all."

"Uh…"

Masamune didn't know what to say.

Mutsumi snorted with laughter.

"You should have written 'art teacher' or something," she said. "You're good at drawing."

Mutsumi's tone of voice suggested she was teasing Masamune, but there was a warmth to her words that made Masamune flinch. Without thinking, he leaned forward and asked, "How did you know I like drawing?"

"…? I didn't know you liked it. I just know you're good at it. We've been in the same class for years."

Something clicked inside Masamune's mind, like something had just fallen into place.

"Yeah… That's true."

"What's gotten into you?"

Masamune wasn't going to hesitate any longer. He looked directly at Mutsumi, entirely sincere, and admitted it.

"I like you."

"…!"

For a moment, Mutsumi held her breath.

The sound of the heater working echoed heavily through the cold, quiet air for what felt like forever, but Masamune wasn't fazed at all.

He'd been aware of his feelings for some time, but acknowledging them had always caused him some pain. At this moment, however, he felt so close to Mutsumi—and he was surprised by how easily he was able to accept his emotions.

But then Mutsumi shot him a cold glare.

"You're so sneaky."

"Huh?"

"Just because you've won me over in the real world, you think you can do the same with the me that's right here…"

She'd hit the nail on the head.

At the same time, though, she'd gotten it totally wrong. Of course, seeing themselves as a couple may have motivated Masamune to express his feelings—but that wasn't all there was to it.

"You must have known. I've…liked you for a long time."

"…"

"I'm sure you knew from the get-go. That's why you took advantage of my feelings…"

"Yeah, I knew. But…"

Mutsumi got up from the stall. She walked past Masamune, and once her face was out of sight, she made a frank declaration.

"I don't like you."

"Mutsumi!"

With that, Mutsumi left the rest area. Masamune didn't hesitate to chase after her.

A faint layer of snow—enough to leave footprints in—had covered the rest area parking lot. Masamune reached out and managed to grab hold of Mutsumi's arm as she ran ahead.

"Wait!"

"I refuse! I mean, you're acting like a total idiot!"

Mutsumi was furious. Her usual phony expression was nowhere to be found.

"But I…," Masamune began, but Mutsumi interrupted him.

"We're different! We're not like those people in reality! We're not alive. There's no meaning to our existence…"

As Mutsumi vigorously tried to shake off Masamune's arm, she lost her balance and fell into the snow.

"Gyah…!"

This made Masamune fall over as well. He found himself leaning over her as she lay on the ground of the parking lot. Masamune winced when he realized how close they were to each other.

"Sorry!" he exclaimed, hastily moving away.

Mutsumi, however, had other ideas.

"Look."

She yanked him toward her chest, as if she were embracing his head.

Masamune ended up with his face buried in Mutsumi's chest, making him flush bright red.

Mutsumi spoke in a surprisingly calm voice.

"There's no smell, is there? That's because it's an illusion."

Caught off guard, Masamune gently bit his lip. He wanted desperately to deny what she was saying.

"That's because of the snow… It gradually absorbs the smells…and makes them disappear…"

"We don't smell because we're not alive."

"But I can feel your heart beating. It's going so fast."

"That has nothing to do with being real."

"You must like me, then."

"I don't."

"That's a lie."

"How dumb are you?"

Snow was softly piling up on top of them. Masamune wasn't cold at all—but that wasn't because he was in an illusion.

"…I feel like spending time with Itsumi has given me the answer to the uncertainty I've been experiencing for so long. When she looks at things, she tries to do so with her eyes wide open. She's enthused by all that she comes across. She's made me realize…that's what it means to be alive."

"…"

"Still, you've taught me something more." Masamune stared at Mutsumi's face. It was so close to his. Their breath was coalescing. It felt hot. The area around his ears and heart felt as if they were burning. The heat was preventing him from feeling the cold—the heat of being there with Mutsumi. "Looking at you annoys me. The things you say play on my mind. I feel irritated, but also excited."

"Masamune…"

"It's not just Itsumi. I feel alive, too. Whenever I'm with you, I get the strong sense that I'm living."

"…!"

Mutsumi almost said something but stopped herself. Instead, she softly touched Masamune's chest.

"Your heart is racing, too."

"Oh…"

The touch of Mutsumi's fingers grew firmer. Her eyes started to well up—proving to Masamune that she could feel the heat, too. It was crazy how intensely they could understand each other, even when they didn't speak.

"There's something that'll make it beat even faster."

Mutsumi's eyelids lowered slightly.

When Masamune saw her long eyelashes flutter, he couldn't hold back any longer. He hurriedly brought his lips to hers. He did so with so much momentum that it made their teeth clack together.

Oops, he thought, but he wasn't going to give up there. He tried to meet her lips once again…and this time, he was successful.

Masamune and Mutsumi were kissing, albeit awkwardly.

This clumsy attempt had the two of them pressing their lips together, as if trying to find the right way to align them.

And on the sidewalk opposite the rest area…

…Itsumi was watching them.

Itsumi had been left home alone that day.

The room was quiet, and the only noise that could be heard was the ticking of the second hand on the clock. Itsumi, who'd been drawing pictures with crayons, suddenly looked up to discover that it was snowing outside.

Captivated by the delicate scene outside—its colors too subtle to be re-created with her crayons—Itsumi slipped on her garden sandals on the veranda and wandered outside.

That's right. Itsumi had simply followed the snow.

When she spotted Masamune and Mutsumi in the parking lot of the rest area, Itsumi couldn't understand what they were doing. She assumed they might have been sleeping in the parking lot—but for some reason, she couldn't bring herself to innocently run up to them like she usually would.

The pair were pressing their lips together—over and over, again and again.

She didn't have a full grasp of what a kiss was or what it signified, but there was one thing she was painfully aware of.

"…I'm being left out."

As Itsumi murmured those words, there was a cracking noise…and fissures started to open in the sky above. An intense heat was radiating from behind the cracks—something foreign to this world stuck in an endless winter.

It was the summer sun.

Under the blazing sunlight, the snow that had been gently falling on Masamune and Mutsumi as they continued to kiss swiftly became heavy raindrops.

"It's…turning into rain," Mutsumi muttered, drenched in droplets of water. They were infused with summer sunlight.

Masamune, meanwhile, didn't react at all. He was too engrossed in kissing Mutsumi.

"Hey. The summer…," Mutsumi began.

"Sorry… I don't want to stop at the moment."

"…Oh."

"…I feel like I'm going to explode."

"Yeah. I feel all choked up…"

Mutsumi and Masamune both knew they were acting really stupid. Maybe this was what people called monkey-like behavior. Still, they were fine with being foolish. After all, they'd been holding back for so long.

They'd been holding back from feeling the summer.

"Oh…"

Itsumi stood there in a daze, drenched by the summer rain. Countless cracks began to form in the overcast sky that had left her mind and body with no escape. A ferociously vibrant summer sky peeked through the rifts above her head.

Meanwhile, Itsumi simply stared intently at the pair who were kissing. She pressed hard against her chest. An emotion she couldn't put a name to was welling up inside, its sharp edge piercing through her.

"Ouch… It hurts…"

Itsumi screamed and the ferocious cracks extended dramatically, the sky shattered—and many strange things happened in different places.

First, the steel factory shook violently. The blast furnaces, which had been operating by themselves since this world began, ground to a halt with a loud creak.

The summer sun against the clouds cast shadows on the ground. Faint traces of smoke drifted from the chimneys, the ground, and the pipes like lingering aromas, dispersing before forming Sacred Wolves.

Odd things were happening at the school, in the shopping district, at the harbor, and even at the bus stops.

The snow turned to rain. The strong summer sunlight shining through the cracks reflected off the roofs and the ocean, making spots shimmer. People gasped at the bizarre yet beautiful sight of winter and summer coexisting.

There was another big change, though. The cracks, which had originally only been in the sky, had appeared all over the town. They appeared in places within reach, exposing how locations looked in reality.

For example, a crack in a traditional Japanese-style building revealed a vacant lot, roped off and overgrown with weeds. In reality, the house's elderly residents had likely passed away, and their home had simply been abandoned and demolished.

Through a fissure that had appeared in an old-fashioned general store, one could see an even older store with shattered windows. Dust had accumulated on the items in the display window, suggesting that the store had been out of business for a long time.

A great deal of time must have passed in reality, but there were hardly any signs of development. In fact, things appeared to have gone backward. These visions of the future were tinged in the hues of summer, lending them a luster that did little to improve the view.

As citizens stared blankly at the scenery around them—distracted by it—the rifts made their way to the people themselves. As soon as someone's right arm became caught in the crack, its edges blurred beneath the summer sky. This was the same phenomenon that Masamune had experienced himself.

"Whoa!" they would exclaim, hurriedly pulling their arms back. At that point, they came to the same, obvious realization.

Illusions were merely mirages. There was no place for them in reality.

The earsplitting sound of cicadas chirping reverberated through the cracks.

Masamune and Mutsumi, who'd been engrossed in kissing, finally realized the situation they were in. Snapping back to their senses, they moved away from each other.

"What the heck…? There are *this* many windows to reality?"

The pair scanned their surroundings before spotting Itsumi on the other side of the highway.

"Itsumi?! Why's she out here?!"

Masamune and Mutsumi hurried over to her, but the girl remained frozen to the spot, a tense expression on her face.

"Itsumi, why are you…?" Mutsumi began.

"I'm being left out," said Itsumi, interrupting her and scowling at the couple. Then she repeated. "I'm being left out."

"What are you talking about, Itsumi…?"

Masamune went to place his hand on her shoulder. She bit his palm as hard as she could.

"…?!"

Masamune tried to pull his hand free, but she kept sinking her teeth in, refusing to let him go. Tears welled up in the corners of her eyes. When Mutsumi saw the look of desperation on her face, she was stunned speechless. It seemed she'd figured something out.

"Calm down, Itsumi!"

By the time they managed to tear her away, Masamune had bite marks on his palm, and his hand was bleeding. Itsumi started tottering away.

"Wait…!"

At that moment, a loud announcement rang out. A vehicle owned by the town council was broadcasting it through its loudspeakers.

The Sacred Wolves have stopped. I repeat, the Sacred Wolves have stopped…"

Masamune and Mutsumi exchanged glances.

"All citizens must head to evacuation sites immediately. Residents of the Shiomi and Yasute neighborhoods should go to Mifuse Town Hall. Residents of the Momose and Ashina neighborhoods should gather at Mifuse Junior High School…"

*

A throng of grown-ups gathered at the town hall that night, leaving no room for the DISASTER PREVENTION MEETING sign. Mr. Sagami sat on a chair at the back of the room with a sullen look on his face, accompanied by a few of his cronies. These cronies varied in age and attire, and they didn't seem to be from the steel factory. Their glaring eyes were fixed on Tokimune, who was explaining the steel factory's stance to the citizens.

"Recently, the Sacred Machine has been operating nonstop, day and night… This is likely due to the considerable number of people who've been wanting to disappear, as the Sacred Wolves were needed to fill the 'holes in their hearts.' There's a chance this has caused an excessive strain on the furnaces…"

At that moment, Mr. Sagami interrupted Tokimune's explanation by loudly sharing his view.

"It's obviously because the god's woman was let out!"

His followers chimed in, shouting things like "He's right!" and "Do you fools finally get it?!"

People exchanged mocking looks, saying, "What's he raving on about?" and "Did he just call us fools?"

Immune to the backlash, Mr. Sagami maintained his superior, condescending attitude.

"Without the Sacred Wolves, it won't take long for reality to seep through the cracks. Unfortunately, our world is already doomed… Oh well," he pontificated.

He looked around at the citizens, but everyone just glared at him in silence.

"Oh well," Mr. Sagami said once more. He took a few steps forward, then looked back at the crowd. Still, no one stopped him. "OH WELL!"

After this final shout, Mr. Sagami left. His followers chased after their leader, calling out to him.

"Wait for us, Mr. Sagami!"

"What's their problem?" said one of the citizens.

The townspeople watched them leave with dumbfounded expressions on their faces. Tokimune was the only one who seemed to be deliberating something.

It was late at night, and Masamune was in his room, packing his belongings into his backpack. If the world he was in was an illusion, it probably didn't matter where he fled. The curtains were drawn, but his room was still fairly bright. It probably wasn't because of the moonlight shining through, though—it was the light seeping through the cracks.

"Can I borrow you for a moment, Masamune?!"

Misato called him downstairs. When he got there, he saw Souji and Tokimune—who had also been preparing to evacuate—looking down at a cardboard box.

"I want Tokimune to see this, too. I was rummaging through the back of the dresser looking for towels we were gifted, hoping to take them with us when we evacuated…" Misato opened the cardboard box, took out a notebook, and handed it to Masamune. "And that's when I found this. There's some stuff about Itsumi written in here."

It was a diary Akimune had kept.

Masamune hesitated for a moment, but then—having braced himself—began to flip through its pages.

August 15th

There was a landslide at the iron mountain. The cracks are severe. That hasn't happened since this world was created.

Found a little girl on a freight train. She had a distinctive smell.

She's really frightened. I caught glimpses of the summer sky through the cracks. I could hear cicadas, too.

The girl came here from reality, on that train.

"She came from reality on a train…?!" Masamune found himself exclaiming.

Souji nodded gently.

"If the machine that carved into the sacred mountain turned into a Sacred Machine, then the same must have happened to the contraption that carried it…"

"Does that mean Itsumi can return if she boards that train?!"

Tokimune remained silent, but Masamune eagerly continued reading the diary.

August 16th

The girl has been put in the rest station inside the steel factory. Ms. Kashiwagi and Ms. Ichikawa from the Citizen Affairs department will take turns looking after her.

Apparently, there was a name tag on the backpack she was carrying. It said "Saki Kikuiri."

At first, I thought it had to be a coincidence, but when I saw the family photo inside the name tag, I was shocked. The guy in the photo, who looked around my age, had a somewhat timid smile that struck me as familiar.

He had a mole on his neck in the same spot as Masamune's. There's no doubt about it.

This girl was supposed to be Masamune's daughter, in a future we'll probably never get to see. She was meant to be my granddaughter.

"That's right. Itsumi…is Masamune's…," Misato murmured, her tone infused with a mixture of affection and pain. Masamune's expression remained tense.

"You knew?" Masamune asked.

His mother gave him a slight nod.

August 17th

I visited the rest station. Unsurprisingly, the girl…Saki really stank.

There's no doubt in my mind that Saki is a real person, from reality. She felt real to the touch. Assuming I'm right, we must find a way to send her back, no matter what.

The issue is whether Mr. Sagami will be willing to cooperate… No, I'm sure it'll be fine.

Beings that come from reality must follow different laws of physics.

We don't know what kind of impact Saki's presence might have on this world.

If she were to grow up, for example…or if she experienced any strong feelings, it could trigger some kind of anomaly in this world.

We need to all work together to find a way to send Saki back to reality. Saving this world might be connected to saving her. I will talk to Mr. Sagami about it.

*   *   *

"If she experienced any strong feelings…it could trigger an anomaly…"

Itsumi was a real person living in an illusory world. The presence of somebody real in a place where nothing was supposed to have an actual form could plausibly pose a world-destroying threat. Akimune's hope had been to save Itsumi, believing that such an act would also save his world…or at least, that's what Masamune thought.

August 18th

Mr. Sagami said he wholeheartedly agrees with my opinion.

But only with the part about Saki's strong emotions causing an anomaly in our world. He says it'd be wrong to trigger such feelings in the god's woman.

That's right. Mr. Sagami thinks the Sacred Machine summoned Saki here…so that she could become its wife, the god's woman. He claims we can't let her escape this world.

Mr. Sagami took Saki to the fifth blast furnace. He says we need to shut her inside the Sacred Machine so that we can preserve this world.

I'm not sure if "preservation" is even the right thing to do anymore…

It sounded like Mr. Sagami had twisted Akimune's theories to fit his own narrative—and driven Itsumi into an even crueler situation.

? ?th

I'm going to stop writing the date from now on.

Counting the months and the days is forbidden. I'd been resisting, but what's the point? It feels ridiculous, writing down a date from late summer while I look at the snow outside.

I didn't want to adjust to this new way of life. But why does it even matter whether I adjust or not? Without physical bodies, we're basically a mirage. We don't live in reality, after all.

That's been on my mind since Saki came.

When I look at her, everything is so clear and distinct.

It's not just because she smells. It's her warmth, her breath. Even her soul, probably. The longer she stays here, the more her outline will start to blur.

Seems like it's not just me who feels like this. Ms. Kashiwagi and the ones who've been taking care of Saki told me they can't take it anymore.

I thought about standing in for them, but Mr. Sagami would stop me. He says no man is allowed to touch the woman of the god. He says he knows someone else who can help.

? ?th

Mr. Sagami brought in his daughter, Mutsumi. She's going to look after Saki in place of Ms. Kashiwagi and her team.

Mutsumi looks a lot like Saki. I feel like she bears some resemblance to the smiling woman next to my son in that photo as well. I asked, and the two of them are in the same class.

I think the woman smiling next to Masamune and Saki might be Mutsumi.

Saki smiled in front of Mutsumi. It's the first time she's smiled since coming here. Maybe I was onto something when I guessed that Mutsumi was her mother.

Mutsumi looked tense the whole time, though. She seems to be keeping Saki at arm's length. Maybe Mutsumi has figured something out as well.

? ?th

I don't feel like going to the steel factory.

I'm reading manga in Masamune's cozy bedroom. I've read this manga countless times before. The character is getting the philosophical secret technique: Energeia, to burst.

I wonder how many times I've read this same panel in this same manga magazine. It's not even that interesting. I know how the story goes. But despite having a vague recollection of the story, I'm fine with rereading it.

I'm trapped in a world that looks the same. It feels like my memory is going downhill.

Come to think of it, apparently Aristotle once said that hope "is a waking dream."

What's the point of this hopeless world, built on the sacrifice of a girl who deserved to see hope?

? ?th

Masamune is drawing again today.

Regardless of how good he gets, he'll never grow up. He'll never carve a future out of it. Despite this, he keeps getting better and better.

Even in this strange world, there's no limit to how much people can change.

That's how I feel when I'm watching Masamune.

Masamune's hands began to shake as he held the notebook.

Right away, droplets started to appear on its pages, causing ink to spread.

"That's right… I've improved. I've gotten better at drawing…" Tears were streaming from Masamune's eyes. "But no matter how good I get… I'll never make it out of here. Still, I've kept drawing every day…and improved my skills."

Masamune caressed the notebook lovingly.

"That made me happy. Improving my skills and being praised for them made me so happy. I don't care if I can't make a future out of it. I'm having fun and experiencing excitement… I'm alive, right here in the now."

But I stole Saki's chances of changing.

*   *   *

"…! Oh…"

Masamune was at a loss for words. Akimune was more dismayed by Itsumi's situation than anyone else.

I can't do it.

Oh, there's light coming from the distance right now. Why is the steel factory always gleaming? These are the kind of ordinary things that have finally started to bother me.

Maybe those are the things I've been deliberately trying to forget.

When you have somebody around who abides by different rules of physics, you can't lie to yourself anymore.

The ground below feels bright, and when I lift my gaze, I can see light shining from my chest area. There are fissure-like things there. Maybe they're cracks. Could humans do this?

Nah. Come to think of it, the sky and the mountains must be illusions, just like us people.

Smoke has come out. They seem to be looking for something.

Oh. They're looking for me.

If I go outside, the smoke will probably plunge down into the cracks in my chest. Then they'll try to fill the rifts in me, just like they do with the ones in the sky.

But then what happens? Can they repair my broken heart? Maybe I'm a fissure in the fabric of this world, for having doubts about it.

I wanted to change like Masamune has. But I just can't. In which case…

From then on, all the pages were blank.

Misato gently patted Masamune's back as more tears fell.

"I hope you will forgive your father, Masamune," she said.

"…It's not about forgiving him."

Masamune used the back of his hand to wipe away his tears.

"I'm just happy he said such nice things about me," he said with a boy-ish expression on his face.

That was how Masamune genuinely felt. He was just glad his father had acknowledged him, no matter how he'd gone about it. Akimune and Tokimune had both been keeping an eye on him, even if they hadn't said a word.

Masamune looked up resolutely.

"Uncle Tokimune…I want to send her back. I want to send Itsumi back to the real world!"

*

"Okay, that's all your stuff. I'll be right behind you."

"All right. Let's go."

Masamune revved up the engine, and the small vehicle with Masa-mune and Souji on board drove away. As Misato watched them leave, she stretched her arms, groaning.

"Okay, next up…"

Tokimune stood in front of Misato, blocking her way. With a tense look on his face, he was staring directly at her.

"Uhh. There's one last thing I have to say to you… Is that all right?"

Misato, having sensed something from Tokimune's passionate tone, averted her gaze and smiled softly.

"Nope. I'm not listening."

Tokimune looked taken aback, which made Misato burst out laughing.

"If everything's about to come to an end, I want to go out as a respect-able mother."

Misato immediately walked past Tokimune and went back inside the house. Tokimune, who'd been cut off before he had the chance to speak, looked rather refreshed by her response.

"I see…," he muttered, looking up.

The cracks, which stretched from the sky down to the ground, weren't being filled in by the Sacred Wolves. Instead, they were spreading in every direction…

Masamune was driving the car down the highway in the direction of the junior high school.

"Oh, you can see so much already."

The coastal highway was full of areas where reality was peeking through. In Masamune's world, it was nighttime, but it seemed like it was still evening in the world beyond the cracks, the darkness tinged with orange. As a result, certain sections of the road where there were fissures had been closed off, leaving only one lane functional. It was unusually congested for Mifuse.

"There was an accident at the steel factory, after all. That's why the place is so deserted," Masamune muttered as he gazed at the scenery through the cracks.

The sun hadn't fully set yet, but many of the stores in the real world had their shutters down.

"It must be the Obon festival," his grandfather said.

In reality, lantern-like adornments were tied up in various spots along the highway.

"You're right. They must still do it, then." Masamune narrowed his eyes as he reached back into his memory. "The Obon festival used to be so much fun. There were fireworks and tons of food stalls. *Yakisoba*, candied apples, target shooting, and candy with embossed pictures in it…"

"You know, I don't think this world was created as a divine punishment," murmured Souji as he gazed out of the window.

"Grandpa?"

"I mean, just look at you."

"Huh? Me…?"

"The god of Mifuse likes being praised… What if he just wanted to take a snapshot of his heyday, when everybody praised him, and preserve it forever?"

As Souji spoke, the winter sea of Mifuse simply shimmered in silence.

Many vehicles were parked on the school grounds, and the grown-ups were carrying in their bedding. There were still glimpses into reality around, but they revealed no sign of life. It seemed like Masamune's school had been abandoned.

"Oh, what happened?" said a middle-aged man, peering inside out of curiosity.

"Watch out!" his child yelled, infuriated.

The curtains were drawn, and the citizens themselves were sealing up the windows with duct tape.

"Try to avoid leaving any gaps! Make sure that no light from the cracks gets in…"

As soon as Masamune walked in through the entrance carrying a cardboard box, he was confronted by a board that had been stuck to the corridor wall. The words *Please divide yourselves up according to your neighborhood* had been scrawled on it in an impromptu fashion.

He stepped inside the classroom. The desks that were usually there had been tidied away at the back, and the place had been completely transformed into an evacuation site.

Mutsumi, Sasakura, and the others had already arrived. They were working on blocking out the light from the cracks, which was coming in through the window.

"Huh? Where's Itsumi…?"

"Hara and the others are taking care of her."

Masamune explained to his friends what he'd gleaned from Aki-mune's notebook.

He told them there was a chance that Itsumi could return to her old world by riding the "train from reality" in the steel factory. He also told them that Itsumi's existence might help preserve the world they were living in.

"If Itsumi experiences strong emotions…"

Mutsumi seemed to have picked up on something.

"But would Itsumi have to take the train to reality by herself?"

"Who's going to drive it?"

As everyone was saying whatever they pleased, loud footsteps approached them.

"No, I don't wanna!"

Itsumi, who'd come running over, suddenly froze when she saw Masamune and tried to turn around to leave. That was when Hara and the others caught up with her.

"Grab hold of her! Her sweat suit got dirty, so I need to change her clothes."

"No, I'm not gonna let you!"

"Come on. You stink."

Itsumi wrapped her arms around herself as if to guard the clothes she was wearing. It was the one Masamune had lent her—the one he'd said looked good.

She turned her face away from Masamune, stubbornly hanging her head. When Mutsumi saw this, she scowled bitterly.

At that moment, the cheery chime of the school announcement system rang out. *Ping pong, ping pong.* ♪

"We have an announcement from New Mifuse Steel Factory. Please assemble in the gymnasium."

"We will run the factory just like we did in reality, using our own power. And then we will intentionally kick the Sacred Wolves into action."

Tokimune spoke decisively as he stood in front of the crowd in the gymnasium.

His unexpected announcement astonished Masamune.

The crowd began to stir. Their cries echoed the doubts that had welled up inside Masamune.

"Wait, what do you mean?" one of them said.

"Didn't you say the world was going to end anyway, Mr. Kikuiri?" said another.

"Yeah, that's right!"

"This isn't what we were told!"

Tokimune, meanwhile, continued without hesitation.

"I understand your concerns. When the Sacred Wolves appear, they won't make much difference. The cracks can't be stopped anymore. This world is going to end eventually… But if we can prolong it for a year, half a year, or even just a single day…" Tokimune locked eyes with the workers, gave a firm nod, then raised his head resolutely. "We won't give up."

"Wha…?"

Masamune was too shocked to speak. The crowd's reactions varied, with some clapping and others merely baffled.

"What's he talking about?"

"That's the spirit, Kikuiri!"

"Come on, I've had enough. This is too much work."

And as for Masamune—his face had reddened with fury.

"Wait up, Uncle Tokimune!"

Masamune caught up to his uncle in the school parking lot as he was getting on his motorbike.

"Weren't you going to help me save Itsumi?!"

"I don't agree with my brother or Mr. Sagami. Personally, I don't think Itsumi will have any effect on how long this world lasts."

"You could have at least waited for her to escape…"

"All I've ever done is wait, even before this world came to be," he replied in a serious tone. Masamune frowned suspiciously, wondering what Tokimune was getting at. Tokimune casually looked up at the sky, as if recalling a distant memory. "Since I was a kid, I avoided conflict… My easygoing brother took everything I wanted. My toys, my pencil cases…even your mom."

"Huh? My mom…?"

"I'm not an object," snapped Misato, who'd just shown up.

Her arrival didn't make Tokimune flinch at all. Turning the key on his motorbike, he made a statement.

"I…don't plan on letting you go out as a respectable mother."

"…?!"

Tokimune zoomed off, leaving Misato and Masamune behind. Masamune, who'd been in a state of stupor, finally returned to his senses.

"What was that idiot saying…? Whatever. I don't need a guy like that to help me!"

Masamune went back into the school, still furious. Misato, who'd been abandoned in the parking lot, stared in the direction Tokimune had gone. Narrowing her eyes, she let out a breathy laugh.

"What an idiot. A colossal idiot, in fact."

When Masamune got back to the classroom, he angrily began sketching a map on the blackboard, the chalk scraping harshly against the surface. It was a map of the inside of the steel factory, showing the position of the train located there.

"She needs to get out of the cracks before that perverted old man brings back the Sacred Wolves!"

"Perverted?"

Sasakura and the others exchanged puzzled looks. Suddenly, a loud ripping sound echoed from the back of the classroom. Itsumi was tearing the tape off the window with a sullen expression on her face.

"Hey, cut it out…," said Masamune. He walked over to her, hoping to put a stop to her bad behavior.

"Itsumi won't go!" she then yelled, bolting out of the classroom.

"Itsumi!"

"What the heck? Doesn't she want to go back to reality?"

"Wouldn't you feel the same way? She's probably forgotten all about her past…"

At that moment, Hara hesitantly spoke up, her voice feeble.

"Hey. If she doesn't want to go back, we probably shouldn't force her."

"What are you talking about? This world is gonna disappear! There's a chance that Itsumi could be saved!" Sasakura argued, expressing Masamune's concerns on his behalf. Masamune, meanwhile, glanced at Mutsumi, unable to shake the unease he was feeling.

"What do you think, Mutsumi…?" he asked—but she didn't answer. Instead, she abruptly left the classroom.

"Mutsumi!"

Masamune hurried after her, but she showed no sign of stopping, striding down the hallway.

"Hey, listen to me!"

Masamune attempted to grab her arm to stop her, but Mutsumi turned around first, seized him by the collar, and pulled him close.

"…?!"

It was a forceful and vicious movement, but it brought their faces so close that their lips could have touched. Masamune tensed up, his heart pounding. Memories of their kiss in the rest area came rushing back—complete with the sensations he'd experienced.

Mutsumi, meanwhile, seemed to have read his mind.

"…Don't get carried away just because we kissed," she snapped.

"What…?"

Mutsumi suddenly let go of his collar. Her downcast expression was tainted by profound regret.

"Itsumi must have seen us… That would explain why there are so many more cracks now."

"Wait, what do you mean…?!"

"I was given the job of taking care of Itsumi…because the god's woman loses her power if she falls in love," said Mutsumi, staring directly at him.

Masamune was rendered speechless.

She can't have…

That's what Masamune wanted to insist, but somehow Mutsumi's theory made sense to him.

He'd never truly felt pain since entering this illusory world, but when Itsumi bit into his hand, the agony had shot straight to his chest.

At that moment, Sasakura and the others came running over. Their faces looked pale.

"Masamune! It's Itsumi!"

"…! What…?"

"Cheers!"

In the classroom, the grown-ups were starting their nighttime drinking party. The members of the Women's Association used supplies people had brought for the evacuation to prepare meals in the cooking classroom, and the products of their labor were being served to the citizens.

"Wait, is that garlic I can taste?"

"I thought it was ginger pork."

Misato, who'd overheard this exchange from behind, laughed as she placed pickles on everyone's tables.

"As long as it looks like ginger pork, there's no real difference…"

"Yes there is," mumbled Souji, who'd been quietly eating his meal. "This is more luxurious than the original."

The same shriek that Masamune had heard countless times before resounded from the television.

"I want to know everything!"

An old man who was in front of the TV turned around to look at everyone.

"Hey… Is this the continuation of that same old drama series?!"

"Huhhh?!"

Everybody ran over, forming an excited crowd.

The woman who was standing before the rain-drenched detective—who was demanding to know the full story—was clearly suspicious.

"Okay then, I'll tell you everything," she began.

It was a scene nobody had ever seen before. People were glued to the TV screen, their hands sweating.

"No way, it can't be her. That'd be too obvious."

"If they've dragged it out this far, there must be a bit of a twist…"

"Yes, the criminal is…yours truly!"

"Whaaaat?!"

Everyone shouted in unison. Soon after, they started voicing their opinions.

"Are you serious?"

"That's too cliché!"

"We should make a complaint!"

"Are you gonna make a telephone call to reality?"

Then a wave of laughter erupted.

"Give me a break. My guess was way more interesting."

"Maybe reality is a lot more boring than our world."

As everyone else was making noise, someone quietly muttered, "If only…we could start over in this world."

Tokimune and the other workers rushed around as the sixth blast furnace glowed red. It seemed to be overheating—perhaps because it couldn't puff out the Sacred Wolves.

"Any normal blast furnace that hadn't been in use for that long would be rusted and stuck…"

But this was an illusory world. The passing of time was ambiguous, so the furnace shouldn't have deteriorated in any way.

That was when a worker came rushing over.

"Kikuiri! That Sagami guy is doing something weird over at the fifth blast furnace…"

"Leave him be," said Tokimune, looking up. "Sagami's unbelievable. From the beginning, he's been determined to have fun in this world…even though a single idea could have significantly changed the future at any point."

A Shinto prayer was echoing from the fifth blast furnace. Dressed as a priest, Mr. Sagami was performing a ritual to quell the god's anger—with his cronies and some elderly men by his side. He was asking for the Sacred

Wolves to be brought back and for the world's existence to be prolonged. In that sense, he and Tokimune were on the same page.

A door slowly opened behind him as he was reciting the prayer. Masamune and Mutsumi peered inside, but there was no sign of Itsumi. When they looked up, they saw that the door to the small room the narrow passageway led to was slightly ajar.

They stealthily climbed the staircase—the sound of their footsteps covered by the sound of the prayer—then opened the door. A modern room stretched out before them with beautiful decorative windows. It was hard to believe they were inside a blast furnace. And there, in front of the old, elaborate silver mirror…

…sat Itsumi, wearing a pure-white wedding dress and a veil.

"So pretty…," Mutsumi found herself saying.

Itsumi shot Mutsumi an icy look. She had a completely different aura than usual. Masamune smiled at her, slightly nervous.

"We came to fetch you, Itsumi."

Itsumi reacted by cowering away. Overwhelmed by the air of rejection radiating from her entire being, Masamune and Mutsumi exchanged glances.

"It was tough. She didn't want to take off that dirty sweat suit."

The voice made the pair turn around. Mr. Sagami was standing behind them, grinning.

"But she chose to be here. She volunteered to become the god's woman of her own accord. Why are you trying to interfere?"

"Stop being so selfish! Itsumi…"

"Mitsumi, I stay here," declared Itsumi distinctly.

Masamune was left speechless.

"You're…quite beautiful," said Mr. Sagami, a relaxed smile on his face. "Your mother was a beauty, too." He glanced at Mutsumi out of the corner of his eye. "But like you…she made a pastime out of belittling me. Not that I care about that after all this time."

Mutsumi scowled at Mr. Sagami.

"My mother never bad-mouthed you to me."

Mutsumi's claim made Mr. Sagami look a little puzzled, but he quickly averted his gaze.

"Th-that doesn't mean anything to me," he said bluntly.

He was acting like an insolent child, and Masamune couldn't help but curse him out.

"Shit. Why was my dad friends with a bastard like you…?"

"Friends?"

Mr. Sagami's vacant eyes started to sparkle, and he suddenly started losing his cool.

"Wait a moment! Did Akimune call me a friend?!"

"Huh?! Why would you care about that?!" exclaimed Mutsumi, kicking him hard in the butt.

This unexpected attack made Mr. Sagami lose his balance.

"Let's go!" said Masamune, grabbing Itsumi by the hand and running away with her.

"I *do* care about that! Answer me! Did Akimune call me a friend…?! Hey, wait up!"

As soon as Masamune, Mutsumi, and Itsumi dashed out into the courtyard, they jumped aboard the train in front of the shrine archway.

"This is perfect… We can take this train and go straight back to reality!" said Masamune.

"Back to reality? But how are we supposed to make it move?" asked Mutsumi.

Mr. Sagami and his cronies were already hot on their heels.

"I dunno! But we can still try to get it moving!"

"This is crazy!"

They jumped into the driver's cabin without any plan. At that moment, the train suddenly jolted.

"Wha…?"

When Masamune and his companions turned around, they saw there was already someone in the driver's seat—a man wearing the steel factory's uniform. It was Souji.

"Grandpa?!"

Masamune gaped at him in a daze, staggered by how heroic the old man looked.

"Hold on tight," Souji said, kicking the train into motion. The train picked up speed, the scenery blurring past the window as the train jolted around.

Just as Mr. Sagami and his cronies were about to surround the train, its loud whistle sounded. They hurriedly tumbled to the sides of the tracks to avoid it.

"Hey! You can't make a Sacred Machine move without permission. You'll be cursed! And not just any curse—it'll be a divine punishment!"

One of Mr. Sagami's supporters turned up in a small truck. Mr. Sagami ran over to it.

"Hurry up and chase after them!" he begged, clinging to the window of the vehicle. "Without the Sacred Machine, there's no getting out of here… Our goal is to take it down!"

"So your grandpa was a train driver. Didn't you know that, Masamune?"

"I think Mom might have mentioned something…but Grandpa never really talked about it."

Souji neither confirmed nor denied it, but his sure-handed control of the train made it seem like he'd been driving it just yesterday.

Itsumi bit her lip hard as she sat in her seat. It was obvious from her entire demeanor that she was not happy with the situation.

"Switch the track points up ahead for me," Souji said, his gaze fixed on a giant lever on the rails. It looked like they wouldn't be able to leave the steel factory without switching and reversing the tracks.

Masamune jumped off the still-moving train and lunged at the lever. It was incredibly stiff, but he used all his body weight to inch it forward, groaning with effort as he did. Somehow, though, he managed to succeed.

"Switching complete!" exclaimed Masamune, unwittingly shouting like a child.

When he got back on the train, Souji smiled and nodded at him.

The train continued onto the switched rails. With his cheeks flushed from the joy of what he'd accomplished, Masamune placed his hand on Itsumi's shoulder.

"Don't worry, Itsumi. You'll be out soon…"

Itsumi, however, aggressively brushed his hand off.

"Ouch!" she said.

"Huh? Where did I…?"

"It hurts! It hurts when Masamine touch me!"

Itsumi was claiming that a simple touch was causing her pain. This left everybody puzzled—but they were soon distracted by a sudden clanking sound. The train shook violently. Their bodies were slammed against the ceiling and the walls, leaving them disoriented.

"Gyahhhhh!"

"Is this a derailment point?!"

Souji looked up. It became clear that Mr. Sagami's followers had deliberately triggered the lever at the end of the rails to derail the train.

The train fell on its side, coming to an unwanted stop. Masamune sat up, holding his head, and called out to the others.

"Is everyone okay?!"

"Y-yeah… Somehow."

They could hear an engine getting closer. Mutsumi, who assumed it was Mr. Sagami and his followers, hurriedly assumed a protective stance over Itsumi—but when a station wagon appeared, they saw that Hara and Yasumi were on board.

"Come with us, Itsumi!"

Hara was driving the station wagon that had raced over, kicking up gravel as it went. For some reason, Yasumi looked uncomfortable.

"Thanks, Hara!" Then to Itsumi he said, "Go on, get in first."

Masamune expressed his gratitude and tried to help Itsumi into the back seat of the car, pushing her long wedding dress out of the way. Just as he was about to jump in with her, the Kikuiri family's small vehicle turned up, with Sasakura and Nitta in it. Sasakura poked his head out of the window and screamed:

"Don't trust Hara, Masamune!"

As Masamune was standing there—bewildered by what his friend was telling him—Hara abruptly started the car.

"Aghhh… H-hey?!"

The station wagon had driven off with Itsumi on board, leaving a dumbfounded Masamune and Mutsumi behind.

"Haraaa?!"

"You stole Itsumiiiiiiii!"

The station wagon Hara was driving jolted violently as it sped around the riverbank near the steel factory.

"Kyah! Your driving is crazy, Hara!"

"Shut up—sorry about that!"

As Hara and Yasumi bickered, Itsumi sat in the back seat, gazing fixedly out of the window. She appeared mesmerized by the Obon festival fireworks display, which was visible beyond the cracks—but the look in her eyes was a somewhat defiant one.

Hara, who'd caught Itsumi's reflection in the rearview mirror, leaned forward and spoke.

"Itsumi. I wasn't saying that loving somebody is painful… I need to correct that."

Itsumi looked up, surprised.

"It *does* hurt, but that's not what loving someone is about. When you love someone…you want to be with them tomorrow, the next day, and even when you're old!"

Hara's words made Itsumi's eyes widen.

"…I know."

She spoke with conviction. At that moment, a deafening honk came from behind them. In the mirror, they could see the car Sasakura was driving speeding toward them, with Masamune and Mutsumi on board.

Itsumi suddenly leaned forward and tried to mess with the steering wheel.

"Go faster!" she demanded.

"Wahhh! Hey, that's dangerous!"

"More fast! More, more, more, more…"

The station wagon was out of control, swerving erratically. It crashed into the small vehicle approaching from behind, making it jerk from side to side.

Masamune and his friends, meanwhile, were desperately trying to hold themselves together.

"Argh! Why would Hara do this…?!"

"She probably doesn't want this to end. In this world, she and Nitta are in love with each other."

"I'm sorry about this, guys," said Nitta.

"Hey, Nitta. Say something to the culprit!"

"S-sure." He managed to open the window—despite all the shaking— and shouted at Hara. "You need to rethink this, Hara!"

"Noooooo!"

"Itsumi!" Masamune called out as the pair were yelling at each other—but Itsumi was covering her ears, slumped forward in the back seat. "Ugh. Can't you go a little faster, Sasakura?!"

Just then, a deep rumbling sound echoed from the distance. It was the sound of drums from the Obon festival.

"Oh, it's getting exciting!" Sasakura exclaimed as he slammed the accelerator, attempting to overtake the station wagon.

At that moment, though, the car he was driving skidded violently, making a loud squeak as it slid and tumbled down a grassy slope.

"Gyahhhhh!"

The sight of this made Hara stop the station wagon. As white as a sheet, she jumped out and rushed to the overturned car. Sasakura was slumped over the steering wheel inside the battered and dented vehicle, and Nitta was lying limply against the passenger seat's dashboard.

"Nitta! You have to be kidding, guys!" Hara opened the passenger door in a panic, but Nitta's eyes were shut and his body was limp. "Don't die, Nitta! No…!"

Hara reached out for Nitta—and then, *yank*. Nitta, who'd been ostensibly unresponsive, grabbed Hara by the arm and pulled his "prey" toward his chest.

"Y-you tricked me…"

Hara turned red, but she didn't fight back. She simply let him hold her. Sasakura, who was in the driver's seat, sat up and let out a weary sigh.

"You still have a little humanity left in you, then," he said.

Masamune and Mutsumi, who had already clambered out of the small car, suddenly heard a strange voice.

"If you don't give back the god's woman, divine punishment will befall youuuuu…"

The small truck that Mr. Sagami and his group were in was hurtling along the other side of the riverbank. Mr. Sagami, who was standing on the luggage rack, was shouting through a megaphone with chant-like inflection.

"The more you resist, the wilder the spirits will become. You'll be cursed relentlesslyyyy, and eventually, destruction will unfoooold…"

Masamune and Mutsumi rushed over to the station wagon. Itsumi was sitting in the back seat, her body stiff.

"Itsumi," Masamune called out, but she simply turned her face away.

"…"

Masamune and Mutsumi exchanged glances, then subtly nodded. Masamune jumped into the driver's seat, and Mutsumi sat in the back with Itsumi. Without delay, Masamune stomped hard on the gas.

The station wagon sped off, with Itsumi still staring intently out the window. She'd been sulking at first, but she'd now become captivated by the Obon festival scenes. She clearly couldn't look away.

The car came to the highway along the coast. In reality, the road had already been closed to vehicles, and there were food stalls scattered around. There were rows of lanterns hanging up, and the festival music was getting louder and louder.

"I never knew that reality could sound so loud…"

"We're out of time. This girl will disappear with us."

Through the cracks, they could see reality. They saw a vivid red circle being drawn in the sky, which was yet to fully darken. Some of it turned green…and shortly after, there was a booming sound.

"Fireworks!"

"Wahhhhhh!"

"Stop it, Itsumi… Ouch!"

Excited, Itsumi had leaned out of the window, her veil fluttering in the wind. Mutsumi tried to pull her back into the car, but Itsumi fought back, making it difficult. Masamune hurriedly hit the brakes.

"Watch out…," he began—but then he froze.

He could see reality through the cracks.

People were sitting or leaning against the seawall, watching the fireworks rising from the sea.

They were drinking alcohol, eating *takoyaki* and simmered squid, playing with yo-yos, and chatting noisily.

But there was one other thing Masamune had noticed. Among the crowd of people enjoying the Obon festival in their own way, he spotted a slightly worn-out middle-aged man walking aimlessly in front of the station wagon…his adult self.

"Oh…"

The version of Masamune in reality was holding a plastic bag. It looked like he'd purchased some small dishes from a convenience store. Despite it being the day of the festival, he hadn't bought any festive food, and he seemed to be avoiding looking at the fireworks. All he wanted to do was go home.

"…It was in my dad's diary," Masamune muttered. "Itsumi came to our world on the day of the Obon festival."

Mutsumi gasped, looking at Itsumi. Itsumi, meanwhile, simply gazed up at the fireworks, her eyes sparkling. Maybe she'd forgotten about the real Masamune.

This was the little girl from reality who'd found herself in the illusory world on the day of the Obon festival.

Perhaps, in reality, we went to see the Obon festival as a family, thought Masamune. *And while we were there, we got separated from Itsumi…*

The real Masamune came to a halt in front of the sugar pipe stall. Then his memories came flooding back. His memories of that fateful night at the Obon festival…

"I want that one!"

That day, Saki had thrown a tantrum in front of a stall selling children's toys that were shaped like pipes and filled with sugar.

"Hey, don't touch the merchandise!"

"I'm not moving from this spot until you buy me one!"

Saki's stubbornness gave Mutsumi an idea.

"Do as you please. Mommy and Daddy are going to move on! Come along, Masamune."

Mutsumi started walking, pulling Masamune by the arm. Saki stayed stuck in place, sulking.

"Uhh, is this a good idea?" Masamune had asked his wife.

"It'll be fine. She's bound to give up and chase after us…"

As she was speaking, Mutsumi felt a wave of apprehension cross over her. When she turned around—

"Saki…?!"

Saki was nowhere to be seen.

A search for Saki was carried out on the festival grounds—but the fireworks were already going off, and they couldn't stop the festivities partway through. Rumors of her disappearance reached some of the rowdy festivalgoers, and one could hear a few murmurs of "A child's gone missing" and "Oh no"—but that was it.

Once the night was over, searching for Saki became the sole focal point of Masamune's and Mutsumi's lives.

Mutsumi became a nervous wreck. It was as though she'd turned into an entirely different person. Whenever Masamune went out alone, she'd worry. Sometimes she'd become so anxious that she'd start to scream. The couple had once talked about wanting a second child, but those conversations faded away. Now all they could focus on was finding Saki.

They scoured every inch of Mifuse, leaving no stone unturned. They made flyers, pleaded for help, and persistently urged the police to continue their search. A day went by, then a week, then a year, then three years…and Saki was still nowhere to be found.

They couldn't find her anywhere…

"Here you go! Your daughter will love it!"

The older Masamune snapped back to the present, looking up with a start. Without realizing what he was doing, he had bought a sugar pipe. It looked like the pipe with the girls' anime heroine on it that Saki had asked for that fateful day. A decade had gone by, and there were different shows on now. The character Saki had liked was probably no longer sold.

For a brief moment, a pained expression crossed the real Masamune's face as he began walking toward the station wagon that the illusory Masamune and his friends were sitting in.

And then he walked straight past his daughter, who was a little bigger than when they'd last seen each other. This was the girl he'd been longing to see for ten years. She'd never left his mind, and he would have given his life to be reunited with her.

As the real Masamune strolled past her, Itsumi blinked in surprise.

"…Masa…mine?"

Masamune watched his real self disappear into the distance through the rearview mirror, then murmured something.

"Here, I'm able to laugh and cry. In this world, I could have been truly free… But it's different for the real versions of ourselves. They can go wherever they like…but emotionally, they spend their days in a state of stasis."

Fireworks burst overhead. Mutsumi looked away from the real Masamune's shrinking figure, a pained expression on her face.

"Yeah… That's true."

"This isn't just about wanting to free Itsumi. I want to set us free, too…the real versions of us."

Itsumi, who was gazing longingly at the fireworks from reality, was hung up on something else.

"Us…," she whispered sadly.

She'd realized that she wasn't part of the "us" Masamune was referring to.

She felt like she was always left out.

At the steel factory, reality had even begun to seep into the sixth blast furnace. The workers, who'd been avoiding the cracks as they attempted to restart the furnace, suddenly found themselves trapped.

"Watch out! If you step all the way into reality, you'll disappear!"

"But we're running out of space to move…!"

"Aghhh… It's all over, Kikuiri! We're done for!"

"It's not over! I'll be damned if I let this end!" exclaimed Tokimune— but as he was shouting this, it began.

Booooom, booooom!

A noise much louder than fireworks echoed through the steel factory. It was the sound of the iron mountain collapsing. At the same time, the massive chimney of the sixth blast furnace started to glow red with heat. Smoke began to billow from various parts of the steel factory—and then it transformed into Sacred Wolves, soaring majestically through the sky.

"Sacred Wolves…!!"

The workers erupted in cheers. Tokimune collapsed to the ground.

"Hah… Ha-ha…"

Mr. Sagami and his crew also caught sight of the Sacred Wolves rising from the steel factory.

"Ahh, our prayers have been answered!"

As his cronies grew excited, Mr. Sagami briefly bit his lip. The Sacred Wolves' return would delay the downfall of the world, even if only slightly. Mr. Sagami knew it was only a temporary fix, a mere drop in the ocean. Even so, there was *something* they could do.

"Now we need to get the god's woman back!"

The Sacred Wolves glided around gracefully, infiltrating cracks all over Mifuse.

The fissures were huge, so the repairs would take somewhat longer than usual. Still, the diligent and committed Sacred Wolves tirelessly continued sealing the rifts, moving from one to the next.

"No… We're not going to make it in time!"

Masamune and Mutsumi were inside the car, speeding toward the tunnel. They were in a total frenzy.

They knew they were illusions, beings who weren't really supposed to exist. But if they could get Itsumi back to reality, it'd at least give their existence some meaning. Even if they were destined to disappear, they were determined to save Itsumi—no matter what it took.

Still, they couldn't imagine making it out of the tunnel in their station wagon. Maybe a Sacred Machine could have done it, but the train had already overturned.

Even so, despite everything—

Meanwhile, in reality, the real Masamune was walking along the railway tracks, making his way home. There, a crowd of people had gathered with cameras. In his world, the cracks linking the illusory world with the real world were invisible, and people couldn't see the fissures being repaired at a rapid pace.

During this Obon festival, the factory—which had been closed due to the explosion—was running its train for the first time in a long while. As the real Masamune watched absentmindedly, he heard a child's voice.

"I want that one!"

A child with their family was throwing a tantrum at one of the stalls, just like Saki had done all that time ago. At that moment, Masamune realized he needed to get rid of what he was holding before he got home. How would Mutsumi feel if she caught sight of it…?

"Would you like this?"

Masamune handed the sugar pipe to the kid who'd been throwing a hissy fit, then walked away without waiting for a reply.

"I don't want this! Mom…"

What the child actually wanted was a glowing bracelet. The kid's mother, bemused, told her child to leave the sugar pipe somewhere.

In the background, a station employee was shouting to the camera-wielding crowd through a loudspeaker.

"The commemorative train is about to depart. Those of you filming the driver's seat, please come out!"

Masamune and his companions, who were driving along the ridge toward the tunnel, looked down at Mifuse as the sound of a train whistle resounded.

"Hey, what's that?!"

They could see a train hurtling along the viaduct behind them, the fireworks from reality reflecting on it.

"A train…!"

"Why?! Who's driving it?"

"No, it's…a train from reality!"

There was still a fissure left, way off in the distance ahead of the train.

"We need to get Itsumi onto that train!"

"But how?! It's on the other side of the crack— Kyah!"

Masamune had stomped hard on the accelerator.

"We'll figure it out!"

As reality and illusion merged, the people in reality could be seen smiling and enjoying the Obon festival, while the evacuees from the illusory world wistfully watched them.

Feeling somewhat relieved, they started looking for familiar faces in reality, the sight of which was slowly fading from view. As they did so, they chatted among themselves.

"Hey, those Sacred Wolves are working really hard."

"It's gradually disappearing…"

"Wait, isn't that the son of the hardware store owner?"

"Yeah, it has to be. He has the same mole."

"Hey, look. Isn't that Mrs. Yamazaki?"

The woman, who'd been pregnant for the whole time she'd been in the illusory world, was walking alongside someone who was likely her daughter. She looked at the real, older version of herself.

They looked more like best friends than mother and daughter. They were laughing together, drinking soda out of strange-looking cups that they'd bought from a stall.

This sight made tears pour down Mrs. Yamazaki's face as she rubbed her large bump.

As the Sacred Wolves filled in the cracks, the image of the close mother and daughter faded, too…

The station wagon that Masamune and his companions were riding in bumped along the rough mountain road. Masamune's hands became sweaty as he gripped the steering wheel. As the vehicle shook violently, Itsumi let out a cheerful cry. "Ooooooooh!" she went. She seemed to like hearing her voice tremble.

Suddenly, their surroundings distorted and the scenery changed. While they were still surrounded by the same green mountains, it was clear that the trees hadn't been looked after. Then a vibrant firework flickered in the sky, revealing a shade of green far richer than any illusion could be.

"We've gone into a crack?!" Mutsumi screamed.

Itsumi looked at her in confusion.

"Is something strange happening…?"

"Huh?"

When Mutsumi glanced at her palm, she noticed that it was blurring slightly. She hurriedly looked up, only to realize that the edges of Masamune's body were also growing indistinct.

They were in reality—a place where illusions couldn't survive.

"Agh… At this rate, we're going to disappear!"

"I know! But this is the only way to get on the train from reality!"

The Sacred Wolves were trying to cover the crack in the sky above the train. Then there was some static…and a muffled noise began to resonate throughout the car.

"This one's from a listener who calls themselves Sleepy Lamb."

The DJ's voice was unique and high-pitched. It was that radio show that Senba liked.

"I've had enough of studying for my entrance exam. Someone help me. I feel like I'm dying.'"

At that moment, Masamune couldn't help but burst out laughing.

"Ah-ha-ha-ha! Is that right? Just go ahead and die, then!" shouted Masamune, chuckling.

"Go ahead and die!" Itsumi cried out cheerfully, following Masamune's lead.

"Hey, that's mean!" said Mutsumi, rebuking the girl like a real mother.

"But that listener doesn't understand what death is like. They shouldn't say stuff like that so casually!" said Masamune.

"We don't know what it's like, either," countered Mutsumi.

"Exactly! And I intend to keep it that way!"

Thwack. Masamune pressed down harder on the accelerator, causing the car to lurch forward.

"Kyaah!" Mutsumi shrieked, protecting Itsumi with one hand and clinging to the front seat with the other.

"It feels like I have no escape right now.'"

The car that Masamune was driving raced up the side road.

"You can find an escape if you look for one!"

"I feel like I'm stuck in an endless tunnel of darkness.'"

Just then, a particularly bright firework illuminated the sky.

"There's always a light that will shine somewhere!"

"But if I get into high school, I'm gonna change."
"You can change even if you don't get in!"
"Masamune, look out!"
That was when Masamune realized he was driving toward a cliff—
"So…I'm begging you, God."
The station wagon flew over the guardrail, diving off the cliff. Before they had the chance to scream, they were plummeting down toward the rail bridge below. The station wagon toppled onto the tracks.
"…! H-hey. Are you guys okay?!"
Masamune's yell made Mutsumi and Itsumi, who'd collapsed in the back seat, lift their heads unsteadily. At that moment, a piercing whistle echoed through the air. The train from reality was hurtling toward them.
"It's gonna hit us…"
Masamune and the others instinctively closed their eyes—but to their surprise, the train came to a halt just in front of them, making an ear-splitting screech.

In reality, the older gentleman who was in the driver's seat of the commemorative train was straining his eyes.
"What's wrong?" asked a voice over the radio.
"Sorry. I thought I saw a car drop onto the tracks…"

Masamune and his companions leaped out of the car. The train had stopped in front of them. This was the ideal opportunity. Masamune pulled Itsumi by the hand, hoping to get her on the coupling segment of the freight car.
"Come on, Itsumi. Quick!"
She shook her head defiantly, not saying a word.
"Please, Itsumi!" Masamune screamed, feeling like he was going to cry, but the girl clung tightly to Mutsumi's waist.
"I not going! Itsumi not going. We stay together!"
With large teardrops welling up in her eyes, she made a desperate plea.
"I stay with Masamune…and Mutsumi! We stay together!!"

"…Oh."

The look in her eyes…reminded Mutsumi of something.

It reminded her of her first meeting Itsumi. Mr. Sagami had called her to the steel factory. When she got there, he'd insisted that she look after her, and Mutsumi and Itsumi had met in the fifth blast furnace.

The girl she'd been introduced to bore some resemblance to Mutsumi herself.

Mr. Sagami's explanation, as well as the name tag and the photo the girl had brought with her, revealed the possibility that she was Mutsumi's daughter from another world. That was exactly why Mr. Sagami had thrust Itsumi on her.

Mutsumi had played it cool, even when she heard the explanation. The version of her in reality was a different person. At first, she thought taking care of the girl would be like a job…but as soon as Itsumi saw Mutsumi, the young girl gave her a soft smile, her eyes still swollen from crying. Maybe she detected something familiar in Mutsumi. At that moment, Mutsumi made a promise to herself.

I can't allow myself to get too close.

If I do, I'll end up loving her.

If that happened, she feared the guilt of keeping the child confined in the steel factory would crush her.

Every time Mutsumi came to the fifth blast furnace, Itsumi would run around, asking her to play. Sometimes she'd intentionally throw a ball at her caretaker. Despite this, Mutsumi continued to ignore her, providing her with only the bare minimum of care.

Maybe Mutsumi's attitude told her something, because eventually, Itsumi stopped expecting anything from her. She stopped showing emotion on her face, and she started playing alone all the time. Since she never got a response when she spoke, she stopped talking. Over time, she started forgetting how to speak altogether.

This is fine with me, Mutsumi thought. *I can't allow myself to grow fond of her.*

One day, after some years had gone by, Itsumi sneezed.

Despite it being winter, Mutsumi could barely feel the cold in her world. She'd presumed it was the same for Itsumi, too. Itsumi had never actually caught a cold.

How did this world's temperature feel to a girl who'd come from reality, though? Mutsumi had never checked, but it was something worth thinking about.

She wasn't used to working with a crochet needle, but she managed to crochet a cardigan for her. Once it was done, she took it to the steel factory and flung it at Itsumi, deliberately pretending not to care about it.

When Itsumi picked it up, she smiled gently at Mutsumi—just like she had on the day they first met…

"Since when did you start calling me by my name?" asked Mutsumi, gently patting her on the head as she recalled the time they'd spent together. Then, looking dazzled and teary-eyed, she made an unexpected declaration. "We'll stay together, Itsumi… I'm going to reality, too."

Masamune looked up in surprise.

"No! If you do that, you'll disappear…!"

Having been in reality for so long, they were both becoming more and more see-through. The trees on the other side, swaying in the night air, looked faint.

"It's only a matter of time anyway—even if I stay in this world."

"But still!"

At that moment, the train started moving again. It must have resumed operation, having gathered that there was nothing out of the ordinary. Mutsumi clambered onto the coupling of the train and reached out for Itsumi.

"Come on, Itsumi!"

Seeing the determination in Mutsumi's eyes, Itsumi instinctively grabbed her hand.

As Masamune watched Mutsumi pulled her up onto the coupling, he shouted, "I'm coming, too!"

He frantically began to run, but the train was starting to pick up speed.

"Mutsumi, I'm coming…"

Masamune reached his hand out as far as it would go, trying to grab hold of the coupling's railing.

Despite his desperate attempts to reach the railing, Mutsumi refused to take his hand. Not only that, but when he eventually managed to catch hold of it, she attempted to remove his fingers, one by one.

"Mutsumi, why are you…?"

Mutsumi glared at him in silence.

"Ah… I! No! I don't want to say good-bye like this… I…I!"

Masamune continued to run. The train was getting farther and farther away, but he just kept running and running.

"—had so much fun…"

Thud. He fell over. As the train sped away, he shouted through his tears.

"…with you guys!"

Mutsumi and Itsumi, who were both so precious to him, were rapidly disappearing into the distance. As he held back tears, unable to stand back up again, the sky suddenly grew dark.

"Oh…"

The cracks in the sky were moving with the wind.

Then he heard a car engine approaching from behind.

"Masamune!"

Masamune looked up, startled—only to discover that Sasakura and his other friends had driven underneath the bridge in the small car.

"The festival fireworks… You can't see the Sacred Wolves from here, then."

As Itsumi and Mutsumi rode through reality on the train coupling, they looked down at the fireworks lighting up the town. Mutsumi's side profile—with her slender, straight nose—was almost completely translucent. The fireworks exploding behind her could be seen through her eyes and lips.

As soon as Itsumi noticed this, she was overcome with fear.

"I'm getting off!" she shouted, leaning forward. "Mutsumi will get off, too!"

When Mutsumi saw the desperate, pleading look in her eyes, she gave Itsumi a sad smile and lowered her gaze slightly. Then she noticed something at her feet and crouched down to pick it up. When Itsumi saw what Mutsumi had found, her eyes widened in surprise.

"…! I…know what that is."

It was the sugar pipe that Masamune from the real world had bought and given to a random child. The child's mother had told them to just "leave it somewhere," so they'd placed it on the coupling section of the commemorative train just before it departed.

"It's a candy pipe. I used to love these… Oh, of course—there's an Obon festival going on in the real world."

Mutsumi handed the brightly colored candy pipe to Itsumi.

"There are loads of stalls, and the fireworks are amazing. It's so much fun. But…here, it's always winter. If you stay here, the Obon festival will never come around."

As Itsumi clutched the candy pipe, Mutsumi spoke gently to her. Fireworks were flickering faintly behind her smile.

"Hey, Itsumi. There's more than just the Obon festival on the other end of this tunnel. There's a whole lot waiting for you out there. Things that are fun, painful, sad… Stuff that will stir all kinds of strong emotions within you."

"…"

"You'll make friends. You'll have dreams. You might experience setbacks, but if you keep going—rolling along—you might find new dreams…"

Fireworks exploded intensely through Mutsumi's translucent chest.

"I'm jealous. All of those things…are things I'll never have."

"…! Oh…"

"So there's just one thing I want you to give to me."

Mutsumi glanced down.

"Look," she said. "You can see Masamune."

The small car Sasakura was driving was on the highway below, careening alongside the train. Nitta, Hara, and Yasumi were all squeezed inside the vehicle. Masamune had opened the window and was looking up worriedly.

Mutsumi gave Itsumi a forceful look, then made a clear statement.

"I'm taking Masamune's heart."

"Huh…"

"You can have everything else——but I'm taking Masamune's heart."

"…!!"

This declaration was so imposing that it left Itsumi speechless. Her fingers and lips wouldn't stop shaking, although it wasn't clear whether she was angry or frustrated.

"Even if I came with you…he'll think of me in this world's final moments."

"No!"

Itsumi covered her ears with her hands. She vigorously shook her head, using her entire body to demonstrate her refutation. Despite this, Mutsumi carried on speaking.

"I'm sure it'll be the same for me. The moment this ends, it'll be Masamune who comes to mind."

"No, no, no!"

"Masamune loves me. And I love him."

"…! I'm left out…"

"That's true. But—"

Mutsumi covered and squeezed Itsumi's hand—the candy pipe still in it—with her own hand, which was nearly transparent. In contrast with the strong words she'd spoken just a few moments earlier, her eyes were full of love.

"There are people who always have you on their mind…and they're waiting for you on the other end of that tunnel."

"…!"

Itsumi stayed still for a while. Perhaps she could feel the warmth of Mutsumi's fading hand.

Then she appeared to arrive at a conclusion—and removed the veil she was wearing.

"Itsumi…?"

She glared defiantly at Mutsumi. With large tears welling up in her eyes…she placed the veil on Mutsumi's head.

"I hate you."

Then she flung her arms around Mutsumi—as if to hide the uncontrollable tears that had started pouring down her face.

"I hate you. So…we can't go together."

"…?! Oh…"

"I hate you."

Itsumi was still holding Mutsumi tight.

The truth was, she'd wanted to embrace Mutsumi like that for a really long time. She wanted to get love and attention from her. The feeling was mutual… In truth, Mutsumi had longed to accept Itsumi in her entirety.

"Yeah… Yeah…"

Mutsumi hugged her back, squeezing her tight as her eyes glistened with tears. In that moment, they could feel each other's heartbeats— giving them the feeling that they were both alive.

"Whoa. There's a whole swarm of Sacred Wolves!"

"Shit. But we're so close to the tunnel!"

The small car was driving under the elevated tracks, chasing after the train. Masamune, who had been gazing up at it, widened his eyes in surprise.

"Mutsumi?!"

Standing on the coupling between the train cars was Mutsumi, wearing a veil on her head. She was leaning forward, seemingly trying to gauge the right moment to jump off. Itsumi was behind Mutsumi, staring intently at her.

"Is she stupid?! What does she think she's doing?!"

"S-Sasakura! Pick up the speed some more!"

"Wait! I'm already going as fast as I can…"

At that moment, a barrage of fireworks shot up into the sky with the intensity of machine-gun fire. They were being launched in reality, which the Sacred Wolves had almost sealed off.

At the same time, Mutsumi spread her arms wide and leaped into the air.

"Mutsumi?!"

Her veil gracefully fluttered open, as if it were her wings. She looked like a butterfly diving into the large flower that had bloomed in the sky.

Itsumi squinted as she watched Mutsumi disappear, seemingly dazzled by the sight.

"Stop, Sasakura!!"

When Sasakura hastily brought the small car to a screeching halt, Masamune jumped out.

Mutsumi tumbled onto a grassy slope and started rolling downward at breakneck speed. Masamune tried to catch her, but she crashed into him, and the two of them tumbled down the grassy hill together.

"Whoa!"

Eventually, they came to a stop, their bodies entangled. Mutsumi, who was lying on top of Masamune in the grass, clutched her head.

"Oww… That hurt."

"What the heck were you thinking, you dummy?! You're bleeding!"

Upon hearing Masamune's rebuke, Mutsumi glanced at her own hand. It was smeared with bright-red blood—the vivid color of life.

"…! Look, Masamune. This is incredible…!"

Mutsumi suddenly grabbed Masamune's hand and pressed it against the wound on her forehead. Then she started to shout, her eyes blazing with excitement—just like Itsumi's once had.

"It actually hurts!"

"Oh…"

"Because you're here! My cells are telling me I'm alive… This world can end today, for all I care."

As she rubbed Masamune's hand against her forehead, Mutsumi gave him an innocent, exultant smile.

"I'm alive right now!"

"Mutsumi…"

At that moment, the pair looked up.

"Sacred Wolves!"

They could see the Sacred Wolves chasing the train. No—they were trying to overtake it. They were trying to fill the crack in front of the tunnel—the one that led to reality.

Itsumi was standing on the coupling section of the train, feeling the wind against her skin. She was looking behind her, gazing blankly at Mutsumi and Masamune.

"Mutsumi."

She could see the Sacred Wolves approaching, but she didn't care. Masamune and Mutsumi, who were in the grassy field, were growing farther and farther away…and the emotions this sight triggered within her were consuming her entire being.

"Masamune, Mutsumi, Masamune."

A single tear traced its way down Itsumi's cheek.

The Sacred Wolves were looming directly in front of her, ready to engulf her—along with the entire train. But then, at that very moment—

"…!"

With newfound resolve, Itsumi swiftly turned to face forward.

With a deafening roar, the Sacred Wolves swept past the train. Itsumi's hair billowed wildly in the powerful wind. Then the Sacred Wolves attempted to repair the countless cracks that had formed just in front of the tunnel's entrance.

Masamune and Mutsumi, who were looking up from the grass, couldn't help but shout.

"Oh no! The cracks are going to disappear!"

"Go, Itsumi! Go!"

While the pair cheered her on, Itsumi kept her gaze fixed directly ahead.

Just as the train was about to smash into the rift that the Sacred Wolves were in the process of repairing…

Gooooooh!

…the train was sucked into the tunnel, aided by ferocious air pressure. At the same time, the Sacred Wolves quietly dispersed.

Before long, stillness prevailed.

"Oh…"

"…They made it."

Masamune and Mutsumi looked at each other and started laughing.

"Ha-ha-ha-ha-ha…!!"

After laughing for a short while, they suddenly fell silent.

The two gazed at each other tenderly, their faces slowly drawing closer…but then Mutsumi abruptly bit Masamune's nose.

"Did that hurt?" she asked, bursting with laughter again.

At that moment, Sasakura and the others came running over.

"You bastard, Masamune! Quit fooling around, dammit!"

Cheers erupted from all over Mifuse.

Over at the steel factory, Tokimune high-fived his companions.

Mr. Sagami, who'd collapsed, had tears streaming down his face.

At the school, Misato and the adults finished off the beer they had left, calling it a "celebratory toast."

Masamune, who was still lying on the ground beside the train, stared up at the sky.

The Sacred Wolves had sealed all the cracks. That was the extent of their work, though.

Despite this, everyone was in fairly high spirits. What they'd achieved so far and what they'd be able to achieve in the future didn't matter.

They felt alive *now*.

It was the first time they'd felt that way in their illusory world.

* * *

As Masamune was enjoying himself with Mutsumi and his other friends, who were all on an emotional high, a question crossed his mind.

What kind of life will Itsumi lead now that she's gone back to reality?

He hoped she'd encounter everything that he and the people he knew were unable to see, touch, smell, and feel—and take all of those things for herself.

It wasn't that he wanted her to experience those things on behalf of him and his friends who were disappearing.

He was simply pleased that she could keep living.

Itsumi had been a bundle of life within a colorless, isolated illusory world. With her fierce light, she'd brought the color back to the world that Masamune and his friends would continue living in.

Even if Mifuse was ending and the remainder of his life was only brief…

…he'd live a life even Itsumi would envy.

At that moment, Mutsumi suddenly looked up.

"What's wrong?" Masamune asked her.

"I can hear crying… Someone's wailing like a newborn baby."

The voice was coming from the tunnel.

Itsumi's voice trembled with anguish, over the top of the roaring train.

"It hurts… It hurts, it hurts… It huuurts…"

She wasn't in physical pain. She just wanted to be with them so much that it hurt.

It hurt so much, and yet she had to leave.

"It hurts… Ahhhh…"

She was crying like a child, large tears rolling down her face. Despite this, she kept her eyes wide open. She shrieked, trying to feel every last drop of pain.

"Aaaaahhhhh…!"

As she screamed, the train plunged through the tunnel. The area that should have been obstructed by a landslide was lying ahead. On the other side, the area seemed to be dominated by blue.

The train sped toward the azure backdrop. As soon as it emerged from the tunnel, a peaceful sea appeared before Itsumi's very eyes—moonlight wavering gently on the water's surface. The faint sounds of barely audible fireworks could be heard echoing from the town.

In that moment, Itsumi turned into Saki again.

*

As she stepped off the train, she caught a whiff of the sea.

An overwhelming light was illuminating the old, neglected roof tiles. The asphalt was still uneven, but there was a certain purity to it. *I haven't really seen anything like this before*, Saki thought. She walked across the empty rotary toward the deserted taxi stand. At that moment, her phone rang.

"Oh, Dad? Yeah, I've arrived in Mifuse… You're such a worrier. I'm fine… Oh, a taxi just turned up. Okay, say hi to Mom for me. Bye."

Saki hung up the phone and got into the rusty taxi.

"To the steel factory, please."

The elderly driver gave a slight nod and then started the car.

"It's been a while since I've had a passenger go to the steel factory. Back in the day, we used to get curious folks who were interested in exploring the ruins, but most of it's been torn down now… Oh, have this."

Without taking his eyes off the road, the driver handed Saki an unusually large piece of candy.

"Oh, thank you…"

She popped the candy into her mouth. It was not only big, but also coated in coarse sugar. It was tricky to move around inside her mouth.

"Well, it's still a creepy place, no matter how long it's been around. I've even heard stories about people getting spirited away over there... Those are just rumors, though. Nothing more than tall tales."

"Oh, I see," Saki murmured, giving the driver a vague response.

The factory grounds were empty. If it weren't for the ropes marking the area, it would have been hard to tell where the site began and ended. As Saki strolled through the blades of grass swaying in the wind, she came upon a restricted area.

Amid the ruins of what had once been the steel factory was the fifth blast furnace. It stood quiet and alone, overgrown with greenery.

Saki's father, Masamune, had been against her coming to this place—but her mother, Mutsumi, had encouraged her, saying, "Go and take a look." Eventually, Masamune had surrendered.

Saki used to live in there. Her memories of that time had mostly faded, though.

"A girl who went missing as a child has returned ten years after her disappearance."

This shocking news created a huge stir at the time, and gossip and speculation were featured in magazines and on the internet. It was the kind of story that sent chills down the spines of parents, evoking disgust or tears. There were even rumors about Saki being raised by animals...

Saki told the grown-ups around her what had happened while she was gone.

She talked about her life at the steel factory, how she'd been raised by a girl who shared her mother's name, and how she'd grown close to a boy with the same name as her father. The adults, however, assumed she was just confused. After all, the factory had been off-limits for the past decade. No one could have possibly lived there.

The police wanted to continue investigating, but it was Mutsumi who asked them to stop there.

"She's come back home safe and sound. That's all that matters."

Naturally, she didn't want to suffer any more unnecessary scrutiny.

That was a major reason why she wanted to close the case. Mutsumi wanted Saki to return to a normal life as quickly as possible, too.

There was, however, an even bigger motive behind this choice.

"I'm sure Saki was loved."

Saki's vocabulary was limited, but she had a wealth of knowledge and huge emotional capacity. Most of all, though, it was her pure smile that suggested she'd been raised with love.

So when Saki—who'd only just become an adult—expressed her desire to visit the steel factory, Mutsumi decided to trust her and accept her choice.

Saki's footsteps echoed as she stepped into the fifth blast furnace.

Unsurprisingly, there was no trace of the time Itsumi had spent there. The place had a shrine-like stillness to it, and a huge amount of light was pouring through its decayed roof.

The dust sparkled in the sunlight. Saki, who'd inherited her love for drawing from her father, had been attending art school since the spring. The memories of her time living in the blast furnace were fading day by day, and she wanted to preserve them through her art. That's why she'd paid the place a visit.

She gently dusted off a step, sat down, and started taking her art supplies out of her bag. The walls and windowpanes were covered in graffiti left by previous visitors—messages directed toward the steel factory, like *Thank you* and *We won't forget*. Some were sprayed on, while others had been written in the dust with people's fingers. As Saki was absent-mindedly looking around, her eyes suddenly widened in surprise.

"…! Oh…"

In a spot softly illuminated by the light, one drawing stood out. It was a sketch of two girls standing close together, and it looked as though it had been scratched into the surface with something.

The girls, who both had serene expressions on their faces, were Mutsumi and Itsumi.

Who had drawn the picture?

Had her father, Masamune, done it after hearing Saki's story? Or…

"…Heh-heh."

Saki let out a small sigh and lifted her head. Her face broke into a joyful, innocent smile—just like the one she used to wear.

This was the place where Saki had experienced her first heartbreak.

THE SAGA OF TANYA THE EVIL, VOL. 1–13

Reborn as a destitute orphaned girl with nothing to her name but memories of a previous life, Tanya will do whatever it takes to survive, even if it means living life behind the barrel of a gun!

Manga adaptation available now!

SO I'M A SPIDER, SO WHAT?, VOL. 1–16

I used to be a normal high school girl, but in the blink of an eye, I woke up in a place I've never seen before and—and I was reborn as a spider?!

Manga adaptation available now!

OVERLORD, VOL. 1–16

When Momonga logs in one last time just to be there when the servers go dark, something happens—and suddenly, fantasy is reality. A rogues' gallery of fanatically devoted NPCs is ready to obey his every order, but the world Momonga now inhabits is not the one he remembers.

Manga adaptation available now!

VISIT YENPRESS.COM TO CHECK OUT ALL OUR TITLES AND. . .

GET YOUR YEN ON!